D1622338

LIFE
AFTER MURDER

NANCY BONE GOFF

LIFE AFTER MURDER

THE MURDER AT MOUNTAIN CREEK

TATE PUBLISHING
AND ENTERPRISES, LLC

Published by Tate Publishing & Enterprises, LLC
127 E. Trade Center Terrace | Mustang, Oklahoma 73064 USA
1.888.361.9473 | www.tatepublishing.com

Tate Publishing is committed to excellence in the publishing industry. The company reflects the philosophy established by the founders, based on Psalm 68:11,
"The Lord gave the word and great was the company of those who published it."

Book design copyright © 2015 by Tate Publishing, LLC. All rights reserved.
Cover design by Roland Caballero
Interior design by Gram Telen

Published in the United States of America

ISBN: 978-1-68164-247-5
Fiction / Mystery & Detective / General
15.07.09

This book is dedicated to my book club friend, Alcyone Mullins. It was she who urged me, on more than one occasion, I might add, to write a sequel to Murder at Mountain Creek. Thanks Alcyone, I'm glad I took your advice.

Contents

1

The Funeral

Jake and Vicky Tillery stood silently, arm in arm, beneath Vicky's less than adequate black umbrella. Rain rolled down the nylon web and dripped onto the grassless soil, splattering droplets of black dirt onto Vicky's navy blue heels and Jake's dark tan loafers. Jake felt sad. New Prospect Cemetery was practically void of mourners. Although the deceased, Stella Hubert, was not his blood kin, she had played a major part in uniting him with his biological father, Dawson Hubert. As Stella's social worker, Jake knew she suffered from a mental illness. Her doctors at Benton Mental Institution diagnosed her condition as paranoid schizophrenic and bi-polar. Due to her suspicious behavior at the scene of her niece's murder, she had spent the majority of her lifetime in the mental institution in Tuscaloosa, Alabama, for the unjustifiable murder of Jake's birth mother, Sudie Newton Hubert.

From beneath the umbrella, Jake surveyed the onlookers. Among those present was Stella's only sister, Ida, and

Ida's husband, Jack. To Jake's pleasant surprise, his father, Dawson; his biological sister, Beth; Beth's daughter, Kayleen; and Dawson's mother, Cora, were also in attendance. Mrs. Tillery, his adoptive mother, had also chosen to attend and had ridden with Jake and Vicky. Jake took the opportunity to introduce her to his newly discovered family. Each of them greeted Mrs. Tillery with the utmost respect. Dawson hugged Mrs. Tillery and thanked her for taking care of his long-lost son and for raising him to be a fine upstanding citizen. The only other person present was a rather large but pleasant-looking woman Jake did not recognize.

Since there was no minister present, Ida asked Jake if he would say a few words on Stella's behalf. Once everyone was gathered around the casket, Jake removed a piece of carefully folded paper from inside his suit pocket and cleared his throat before beginning to read. In the distance, angry thunder rumbled loudly like the beating of a hundred bass drums. Black clouds rolled across the sky like tumbleweeds being tossed by the wind across a dry dusty desert. Seconds later, lightning streaked the darkened sky. The impending storm was close at hand. Jake began to speak.

"We are gathered here today to pay our respects to a woman, who for many years, was thought to be a cold-blooded killer. Indeed, Stella Hubert lived with demons only she could hear. It was those very demons that turned her from a mentally challenged human being to a believed-to-be demonic murderer. Unfortunately, she spent the majority of her life confined to Benton Mental Institution for a crime she clearly did not commit.

"I met Stella only a few short months ago. However, I will be forever indebted to this special lady for helping me find my birth father and the family I never knew existed. I believe it was by the grace of God that Stella's case was assigned to me. Not only did I find my family, I was partly able to solve the murder of my mother and, above all, prove Stella's innocence. There were times when even Stella doubted her innocence. She worried that God would not allow her into heaven. Thankfully, before she passed, I was able to assure her she was not the one who had killed her niece, Sudie. I believe I can truly say that Stella will forever know peace and comfort with our Savior. Rest in peace, dear lady. You will be missed by your loved ones and friends."

Jake refolded the paper and placed it back inside his coat pocket. "Now let us bow our heads and repeat the twenty-third Psalm."

> The Lord is my Shepard: I shall not want.
> He maketh me to lie down in green pastures: He leadeth me beside the still waters
> He restoreth my soul: he leadeth me in the paths of rightousness for his name's sake.
> Yea, though I walk through the valley of the shadow of death, I will fear no evil: for thou art with me; thy rod and thy staff they comfort me.

Thou preparest a table before me in the presence of mine enemies; thou anoinest my head with oil; my cup runneth over.
Surely goodness and mercy shall follow me all the days of my life; and I will dwell in the house of the Lord forever. Amen

When the prayer was finished, Jack placed his hand beneath Ida's arm to steady her, then helped her over to her sister's casket. Tears rolled down Ida's pale wrinkled face as both she and Jack placed a single red rose on top of the drab-grey coffin. The woman Jake did not recognize waited until Ida and Jack moved away before placing a single white peace lily on the casket next to the two roses. The only other flowers at the grave site were a spray of pink carnations Jake and Vicky purchased from the local florist.

Rain began to come down harder. The sky grew darker. Thunder rumbled overhead and a fierce bolt of lightning pierced the sky, mimicking the loud crack of a whip. Everyone said their last good-byes and quickly headed for their cars. Jake reached the car first and hastily opened the doors. Vicky slid onto the front seat and handed Jake the umbrella. Mrs. Tillery slid onto the rear seat. As Jake was closing the car doors, the unidentified woman touched him on the shoulder and spoke to him for the first time.

"Mr. Tillery?" she asked, more as a question than a greeting.

Jake turned to face her. She was wearing a dark blue raincoat with the hood pulled over her head.

"Yes, I'm Jake Tillery," he said, extending his hand to her.

The woman shook Jake's hand. "May I have a word with you?"

Jake smiled. "Yes, of course. But let's get inside the car where it's a bit drier."

She and Jake walked around to the other side of the car. Jake opened the rear door and the lady slid onto the seat beside Mrs. Tillery. Jake closed the rear door, opened the driver's side door, closed the umbrella, and quickly slid beneath the steering wheel. Despite the umbrella, the blowing rain had managed to creep beneath it, leaving his trousers and shoes soaking wet from the knees down. When he was settled in, he turned to the woman sitting in the backseat.

"I don't believe I know you," he said.

The mysterious woman pulled her hood away from her face, revealing her chocolate ice cream complexion, chestnut-colored eyes, and shiny black hair. However, Jake could tell she was an older woman by the gray hair beginning to peek through at her temples and the deep-set wrinkles in her face. She smiled, and when doing so, her eyes revealed a woman full of compassion for those around her.

"My name is Bernice Stapler. I was Stella's nurse while she was at Benton Mental Institution. She and I became very close over the years. When I heard she had died, I wanted to pay my respects."

"I know Stella would appreciate you being here," said Vicky.

Bernice nodded her head and continued her story. "I know Miss Stella had some mental problems, but she was kind too. She befriended a young girl by the name of Rose. Rose had Down's syndrome. Most people found her to be a pain, but not Miss Stella. After a while, Rose began to call her Mama. They loved each other dearly."

Jake nodded his head in agreement. "Stella spoke to me about Rose. She missed her very much."

"When Rose died, Miss Stella made me promise she too would be buried in the pauper's cemetery next to Rose. When I heard about Miss Stella's death, I didn't know what to do. I called Miss Ida, but she said she didn't have the money to have her body transported to Tuscaloosa. I feel real bad about not being able to keep my word to Miss Stella. I thought you might be able to help me."

Jake thought for a moment. "I don't think they would allow Miss Stella to be buried there anyway. Once people leave the hospital, the facility is no longer required to be responsible for burying them. However, there might be a way we can move Rose here to New Prospect Cemetery. If I'm not mistaken, the lot on which Stella is being buried was purchased some years ago when she and her estranged husband, John, were still married. Perhaps I can get in touch with him to ask if he would let Rose's body be moved and laid to rest by his ex-wife. I think he owes Stella that much."

Bernice seemed pleased. "That would be real nice, Mr. Tillery. I know Miss Stella would rest better if she had Rose there beside her. In fact, I've got a little money saved up and would like to donate it to help pay for the expenses of having sweet little Rose moved here."

Bernice reached into her black patent-leather purse and pulled out an envelope. Inside it were five twenty-dollar bills. She handed it to Jake. Jake started to refuse the money, but Bernice insisted he take it. He thanked her and placed the envelope in his coat pocket.

"I can't promise anything for sure, Mrs. Stapler, but I promise I'll do my best."

"That's all a body can ask, Mr. Tillery."

Bernice reached for the door handle.

"Can I drop you off somewhere?" Jake asked.

"No thank you. My car is parked on the other side of the church. I'll be fine."

"Well, at least let me drive you over there. The rain is getting harder by the minute, and I'd hate for you to get struck by lightning."

Bernice looked out the car window. As if on cue, a bolt of lightning lit up the sky and struck a nearby tree, causing it to split in half.

"Well, all right then," she agreed, "that's mighty kind of you. The rain is coming down pretty hard and that poor tree is certainly ruined." She reached in her coat pocket, took out a small white handkerchief with dainty pink roses embroidered along the edges, and dabbed at the tear running down her cheek. "My mama used to say, when it rained on a day someone was buried, it meant the angels were crying."

Jake put the key in the ignition, put the car in gear, and drove slowly toward the church. "Well, if that's the case," he replied, "all of heaven must be crying today."

When Jake reached Bernice's car, he stopped as close to it as possible. She thanked him again, pulled the hood over her head, opened the car door, and made a mad dash for her own car. Once she was safely inside and the car's motor was running, only then did Jake pull away and back onto the main two-lane road. As he drove away, he looked in his rearview mirror. Bernice steered her car across the rain-soaked parking lot and then pulled onto the road going in the opposite direction.

"She seems to be a nice lady," said Vicky. "She and Rose were probably one of the few friends Stella had in that awful place."

Jake's heart felt a twinge of pain as he remembered the night he told Stella about her innocence. She looked as though the weight of the world had been lifted from her shoulders. To be institutionalized for something you didn't or couldn't believe you could do must have been a nightmare for her. Now he had been asked to fulfill her wish to be buried by her friend, Rose. How he was going to go about it was unsure. What he did know was he owed it to Stella to do everything he could to see her wish come to pass even if he had to pay for it himself.

Jake had been working as a social worker for Jefferson County for nearly twenty years. In fact, that was how he first came in contact with Stella Hubert. In doing so, it had led him to finding his biological family, which he had been told were killed in a car accident. Along the way, he learned his real mother had been murdered while pregnant. The killer had cut Jake from her womb with a hatchet, stuffed him in his jacket, and later sold him to the Tilleries. On his first birthday, Jake was legally adopted and became their only child.

The morning after Stella's funeral, Jake arrived back at his job earlier than usual. He needed to make several calls to see if he could, in fact, move Rose from her resting place in the pauper's cemetery to the graveyard in Marbury. His first call was to the administrator at Benton Mental Institution. He was told there shouldn't be a problem in moving Rose's body as long as it didn't cost the facility any money. That was exactly what Jake figured he would say. Finding the whereabouts of Stella's ex-husband, John, wasn't going to be quite as easy.

The first thing he tried was directory assistance but with no success. As he was about to go online to do a search, his phone rang. He looked at his watch. It read a quarter till nine. Office hours didn't start until nine, so he thought about letting the answering service get it. However, after the third ring, he picked it up.

"Hello, this is Jake Tillery. How may I help you?"

To his surprise, it was Vicky.

"Hi, honey. Sorry to bother you at work."

Jake smiled and leaned back in his chair. "No problem. What's up?"

"I just wanted to let you know I have to be in Huntsville today to cover the governor's visit to the space center. I'll probably be gone most of the day. What's on your agenda for today?"

"Well, I made a call to Benton Mental Institution and was able to talk to Mr. Poole, the sanatorium administrator. Just as I figured, they don't have a problem with us moving Rose, but they certainly aren't willing to fork out any money to help pay for the move."

"That doesn't surprise me."

"No. Me either. When you called, I was trying to find out how to get in touch with John Hubert. I called the phone company, but they don't have a listing for him."

"Why don't you call your dad? After all, Mr. Hubert is his uncle. I'm sure he would know where he can be reached."

Jake laughed. "Now I know why I keep you around," he teased. "Great idea."

"Glad I could help. Listen, I've got to get on the road if I want to get set up in time for the governor's speech. You have a good day. I love you."

"Yeah. You be careful driving up there. I love you too. Bye."

"Bye. Talk to you later."

After hanging up the phone with Vicky, Jake immediately dialed his dad's number. It was answered on the third ring. The voice of his teenage niece, Kayleen, was immediately recognizable.

"Hello."

"Hi, Kayleen. It's Jake. How are you this morning?"

Kayleen smiled. "Hi, Uncle Jake. I'm fine. What a surprise hearing from you so early in the morning. I hope nothing is wrong."

Jake still wasn't used to being called uncle. *It has a nice ring to it*, he thought.

"Nothing's wrong. I just needed some information about the whereabouts of John Hubert. Do you or your grandfather know where I can get in touch with him?"

"That might be a little difficult. You see, he died several years back."

"Oh. Sorry to hear that. Do you happen to know where they buried him?"

"Yes. He was buried here in Montgomery at Greenwood Cemetery next to his second wife. I didn't even know he was married before Aunt Debra. That is until all this came up about the murder and all. Why do you want to know the whereabouts of Uncle John?"

Jake explained to Kayleen about the conversation he'd had with Bernice Stapler and about the promise she'd made to Stella.

"Wow. And you're gonna try and get Rose moved next to Stella?"

"Yes, if at all possible. When I was making arrangements for Stella's funeral, I discovered Uncle John purchased two plots at New Prospect, so the one beside Stella should still be available."

"That is so sweet of you to do this for Miss Stella. You're such a nice person, Uncle Jake. I'm so glad you're a part of our family now."

Jake felt a lump forming in his throat. "Me too, Kayleen. Me too. Listen, it was good talking to you, but I'd better get off this phone before they fire me for making a personal long distance call. Tell everyone I said hello and give them my love. I'll be in touch soon. Bye now."

"Bye, Uncle Jake. I love you."

"I love you too, Kayleen. Bye."

Jake hung up the phone and a wide smile came over his face. How blessed he felt. As he was looking up the number for Jerry Cook, the gentleman in charge of the New Prospect

Cemetery, his supervisor, Geraldine Porter, knocked on his office door. Jake looked up from his Rolodex. "Come in."

Geraldine opened the door, peeked inside, but did not enter. "Good morning, Mr. Tillery. When you get a minute, I need to see you in my office."

Although Jake knew having a meeting in Mrs. Porter's office usually meant another difficult case to deal with, he readily answered, "Yes, certainly. Give me five minutes or so."

Geraldine raised her dark, close-set eyebrows as though being put off for five minutes was an unforgivable inconvenience. "Five minutes. No more. This is important."

Jake raised his open hand indicating five minutes and mouthed the words, "Five minutes."

As soon as Geraldine closed his door, he continued flipping through the rolodex until he found Jerry Cook's name. Dialing the number, he put the receiver to his ear and leaned back in his chair. After several rings, a man's raspy voice answered the phone.

"Cook residence."

"Mr. Cook, this is Jake Tillery. I talked to you earlier when I was making arrangements for Stella Hubert's burial."

Mr. Cook cleared his throat. "Yeah, I remember ya, Mr. Tillery."

"I hate to bother you, but I need some information about the plot belonging to John and Stella Hubert. You said it was a double plot. Is that correct?"

"Yeah. John Hubert bought a double plot back when we first cleared land for the cemetery."

"Good," Jake answered. "As you may or may not know, John Hubert passed away some time back and was buried in Greenwood Cemetery beside his second wife."

"Well sir, I wondered what happened to him. I knew he died, but nobody ever contacted me 'bout his plot so I figured as much."

"Anyway, I have a proposal to make to you." Jake explained the situation concerning Rose and Stella to Mr. Cook. "Do you think moving Rose and laying her to rest beside Stella would be a problem?"

Mr. Cook was silent for a moment. Jake could hear Mr. Cook rubbing his rough calloused hand across his day-old bearded chin. Finally, he answered, "Well, Mr. Tillery, we don't usually bury folks in New Prospect Cemetery unless they're members of our church. I'll have to speak to the other deacons. I don't have no problem with it, but I ain't got the last say-so. Ya give me a number where I can reach ya, and I'll let ya know what we decide."

Jake gave Mr. Cook his home and work phone numbers, thanked him for his time, hung up the phone, and hurried to Mrs. Porter's office.

The door was slightly ajar. He knocked on the casing and peeked inside. Mrs. Porter was sitting at her desk reading some paperwork. She looked up and saw it was Jake and immediately looked at her watch. Ten minutes had passed since their original conversation. She laid the papers on her desk and, with one raised eyebrow and a rather aggravated look on her face, tapped on her watch indicating the lapse of time.

Jake walked across the room and took a seat in the chair directly across from her desk.

"Sorry I'm late. Had to make an important phone call."

Mrs. Porter removed her dark-rimmed reading glasses and placed them on her desk. "I do hope it was a call concerning one of your clients."

"Yes, it was. Absolutely."

"Fine then, let's get down to the reason I wanted to speak to you."

Mrs. Porter pushed a file across her desk toward Jake.

Immediately, Jake began shaking his head. "Mrs. Porter, you must know I can't take on another client. I'm already overloaded with cases."

"Now, Mr. Tillery, you must understand. With the hiring freeze, everyone is having to take on more cases than they would prefer to handle. There is nothing I can do about that. Since you are one of my best workers, I felt you should be the one to handle this case. His name is Judas S. Solomon. He has been an inmate at Kilby Prison for the last twenty years. He is being released tomorrow. He has no family, and because of his age and his criminal record, it is highly unlikely he will be able to get a job. Therefore, he will need our services. You will need to find him a place to live, set up a food stamp program for him, and get him on financial aid."

Jake thumbed through Mr. Solomon's file. "Well, ain't that a kicker? He's been fed, clothed, and housed by the state for the past twenty years. Now he gets fed, clothed, and housed by the taxpayers for the rest of his life. And it says here he was sentenced to life for the beating and murder of a twenty-two-year-old woman. What I want to know is, why he's being released in the first place?"

"The state claims the prison is overcrowded. Therefore, he is being released on good behavior. It seems while he has been incarcerated, he has become a born-again Christian." She paused. "Everyone deserves a second chance, Mr. Tillery."

Jake looked up from the file. "Would you think he deserves a second chance if it was your daughter he killed?"

Mrs. Porter had no answer for his question. "That is beside the point. Whether you or I think he should still be in prison is irrelevant. The fact is, the state is releasing him, and it is our job to see to it that he is taken care of. He will still have to report to his parole officer. And who knows, maybe he has turned over a new leaf. Who are we to judge?"

Jake replied sarcastically, "Well, I know I'm certainly at ease knowing there is a known killer out there who may or may not have turned over a new leaf."

"Deciding whether or not to release a prisoner is not your job, Mr. Tillery. You know what your job is, and I expect you to carry it out to the best of your ability."

Jake rose from his chair, stood at attention, and saluted Mrs. Porter. "Yes, ma'am!"

As he turned and headed for the door, Mrs. Porter called after him, "And I can do without your less-than-perfect attitude, Mr. Tillery."

Jake did not reply. He felt very deeply about hard-core criminals being let out of prison on so-called good behavior. Way too many times he'd seen men and women alike being released only to commit the same offense they were put in prison for in the first place; sometimes even worst offensives than the first time. He would try to give the Solomon fellow the benefit of the doubt, but it wasn't going to be easy.

Jake went back to his office. Several clients were already seated in folding chairs along the wall outside his office; one of which was Mrs. Peacock. She was an elderly lady who absolutely adored Jake. Upon seeing him, she rose to her feet.

"Hello, Jake honey. Are you ready for our wedding today?"

Mrs. Peacock talked about Jake and their impending marriage to anyone who would listen. She was obsessed with the two of them getting married.

Jake smiled. "Not today, Mrs. Peacock. Maybe next time. How are you doing?"

"Oh…I'm as fine as snuff and not half as dusty," she replied, batting her eyelashes and running her faux-diamond, ring-covered fingers, along the pink lace neckline of her hot pink dress.

"That's wonderful, Mrs. Peacock. How about you have a seat out here so I can visit with Mr. Jones and Mrs. Hall for awhile. I'll call you when it's your turn. Okay?"

"Well, okay, but don't take too long. The preacher will be here shortly so we can get hitched."

Jake helped Mrs. Peacock back to her chair and then motioned for Mr. Jones to enter his office. The rest of the day was spent seeing one client after another. The time flew by quickly, and before he knew it, the day was finished. Just as he was about to leave, the phone rang. He thought not to answer it, but he hoped it might be Mr. Cook calling back.

"Hello. Jake Tillery."

"Hello, Jake Tillery. This is Mrs. Tillery."

"Hi, Vick. What's up? I was just on my way out the door, headed for home."

"Well, I was wondering if you'd like to meet me somewhere for dinner. I've had a really busy day, and I don't feel like cooking tonight. Besides, I have something I need to tell you."

"Dinner out sounds good. How about Martini's?"

Martini's was a local restaurant just around the corner from Jake's office.

"Martini's is fine with me. I should be there in about ten minutes."

"Great. See you there. Oh, by the way, what is it you want to tell me?"

"Never mind. I'll tell you when we get to the restaurant."

"Okay. Be careful. Love you."

"Love you too. See you shortly."

2

A Wonderful Surprise

Jake drove the short distance to Martini's and parked in the nearest parking space. Although it was only a few minutes after five, the parking lot was already nearly full. While he was waiting for Vicky to arrive, he reached for the file on Judas Solomon. On the first page was a picture of Judas. It was hard to know when the picture was taken, but by the looks of him, he had led a very hard life. His face was furrowed with deep-set wrinkles. The thing that caught Jake's attention was his eyes. His eyes had the look of evil in them, blank and without feeling. As Jake began reading the police report about the murder of twenty-two-year-old Marsha Hide, his stomach turned over, not from hunger, but from repulsion. The details of the murder were nauseating. She had been shot and her head beaten beyond recognition. A knock on his window made him jump. He looked up and put his hand to his chest. He saw it was only Vicky. She started laughing. He opened the door.

"You scared me."

Still laughing, Vicky replied, "I'm sorry. I didn't mean to scare you."

Jake threw the file he was reading on top of the others, got out of the car, and kissed his wife on the cheek. "And you are laughing, why?" he asked, jokingly.

"You should have seen your face. Call it payback for all those times you've sneaked up on me and scared the living daylights out of me."

"Fine then. We'll call it even. Let's go in. I'm starved."

Dennis Martini, owner of the restaurant, was a friend of the family. They'd known each other for years. Dennis was coming from the kitchen just as Vicky and Jake came through the door.

"My good friends," he called to them in his loud Italian accent. "Come in! Come in!"

Vicky hugged Dennis and Jake shook his hand.

"So glad you two are here tonight. The specialty for the evening is one of your favorites, veal Parmesan."

Jake and Vicky looked at one another and smiled. Jake said the Veal Parmesan sounded good to him. Vicky agreed. Dennis directed them to Vicky's favorite table next to the huge fish tank full of tropical fish. Vicky loved watching the colorful fish swim in and around the artificial shipwreck. Their colors were so brilliant and beautiful. However, that night she did not seem the least bit interested in the fish tank. Sitting across from one another, Vicky reached and took Jake's hand, holding it gently.

"Jake."

"Yes."

"I don't know how to tell you what I need to tell you," she said giddily.

"What? Just tell me. As long as you're not telling me you want a divorce, I can take it."

"Don't be silly, Jake. Divorce is the furthest thing from my mind."

"Well, just spit it out. You got a new job. You won the Pulitzer Prize for journalism. What? Just tell me."

Vicky smiled and a tear rolled down her cheek. "Jake, you're going to be a daddy."

Jake fell silent. He was in shock. They had tried to get pregnant for twenty years. After trying for so long, the doctors had told them Vicky would never get pregnant, and they should adopt. They had talked about adopting, but with both their busy schedules, it seemed they just never had time to follow up with it.

"Jake. Did you hear what I said? We're pregnant."

Jake stuttered. "A-a-are you sure?"

"Yes, dear, I'm sure. I went to see my gynecologist first thing this morning, and he confirmed it. I was dying to tell you before I left for Huntsville, but I didn't think telling you on the phone was appropriate."

"But I thought—"

"No one was more surprised than Dr. Alford."

Jake sat staring into Vicky's eyes. A knot formed in his throat. Dennis came to the table with their dinner just as a tear escaped from Jake's left eye and rolled down his cheek. Vicky let go of Jake's hand so Tim could place the plates of steaming hot Veal Parmesan on the table. When Dennis saw the look on Jake's face, he became troubled.

"Jake, are you all right?" he asked.

Slowly, Jake looked up at Dennis and a wide grin filled his face. Up he jumped, knocking over his chair in the process. He grabbed Dennis on either side of his shoulders and began jumping up and down like a little kid.

"We're pregnant!" he shouted. "We're gonna have a baby! Can you believe it, Dennis? I'm gonna be a daddy."

Dennis grabbed Jake around the neck and began jumping up and down with him. Vicky sat there laughing at both of them. Suddenly, everyone in the restaurant began clapping. A couple of the waiters whistled loudly. Dennis pulled away from Jake's grip and leaned over to hug Vicky.

"Congratulations, Vicky. I am so proud for you both. You will make fine parents. That is, if you can get your husband to stop jumping around like a madman."

Jake vigorously shook hands with several people seated at the tables next to theirs. After a few minutes, he finally settled down and went back to his seat. He looked lovingly across the table at his wife. "We're going to be parents, Vicky."

"I know, Jake, but we have to talk about this. We have some decisions to make. After all, I am thirty-nine years old. Sometimes there are problems involved when carrying a baby at my age. There is a higher chance of it being born with defects. We have to consider whether or not we are willing to take the chance of having a baby with a chromosomal disorder like Down Syndrome or nonchromosomal defects like gestational diabetes, preeclampsia, and intrauterine growth retardation."

Jake immediately became serious. He reached across the table and took both of Vicky's hands into his. "Listen to me, Vicky. God did not allow us to get pregnant after all these years just to give us a defective baby. Our baby is going to be perfect in every way. He or she is going to be as beautiful as you are." He paused for a moment. "And even if we happen to have a baby with a defect, we will love it just the same because it is a part of us, and it is a gift from God. No gift from him is ever wrong."

Now it was Vicky's turn to cry. Jake took his handkerchief from his back pocket and handed it to her. Vicky used it to dry her tears, blew her nose, and tried to hand it back to Jake. To lighten the moment, he pulled his hands away. "No way. You keep it now. I don't want that old snotty thing with boogers all over it."

Vicky laughed.

Now that Jake was over the shock of becoming a daddy, he remembered how hungry he was. "Let's give thanks and then eat this yummy looking food!" he exclaimed.

Vicky agreed. They bowed their heads and held hands across the table. Jake said grace. "Dear Heavenly Father, we thank you for this food we are about to eat. We thank you for the blessings you bestow on us every day. We especially thank you for this latest blessing. We ask, Lord, that you grant us a healthy, happy baby, and above all, the knowledge to raise our child to be a good person. Amen."

With that said, they picked up their forks and began eating like they hadn't eaten in a week. Jake looked over at his beautiful wife and thought about the new life growing inside her. "Thank you, Lord," he whispered again.

Jake could hardly wait to tell the family about the baby. Although he had recently found his biological family, he still had his adoptive mother. She and his adoptive dad were the ones who had raised him. His father had passed away some time ago, but unlike his real mother, his adoptive mother was still living. He loved her very much and wanted her to be the first to know. Jake suggested they drop by her house on the way home from the restaurant. Vicky wholeheartedly agreed.

They got to Mrs. Tillery's house around eight in the evening. The only lights on in the house were in the den. In Jake's mind, he could see his mother sitting in her favorite recliner, nodding off to sleep while attempting to watch the end to some show on television. He remembered how his dad used to tell her she should go to bed if she was that sleepy. She would say she wasn't asleep, just resting her eyes.

Jake took Vicky by the hand, and together, they walked up the long walkway to the front door. As they were walking, Jake thought about the day, not so long ago, when his mother told him about the night his father brought him to her. He had not always known he was adopted. They had told him when he turned sixteen. However, they had also told him his real parents were killed in a car accident, which was not the case. Only after showing her the composite drawing his friend, FBI agent Russell Andrews, had drawn, which turned out to look exactly like Jake, only then did she tell him the truth.

She told him about being wrapped in a bloody jacket alongside a figurine of a dancing ballerina. She told him how her husband had refused to tell her where he'd came from, only that he was a gift from God. She explained how she searched the newspaper every day for some clue as to his real identity and how, after a while, she convinced herself he had indeed been a gift from God.

When he and Vicky got to the door, Jake reached for the doorknob, but Vicky stopped him.

"Don't you think we should knock first?"

"Why?"

"We don't want to scare her by just popping in."

Jake thought about it for a few seconds and decided perhaps she was right. His parents had lived in the same house ever since he could remember, but they had never installed a doorbell. Mr. Tillery always said a doorbell was a waste of money because that was what knuckles were for—to knock on doors. So Jake knocked. He could hear his mother scuffling down the hall. Before opening the door, she pulled back the shade covering the window on the upper part of the door. When she saw it was Jake and Vicky, she smiled, quickly unlocked the door, and opened it to greet them.

"What a surprise! What are you two doing here this time of night? You should have told me you were coming, and I could have made us some tea. Would you like some tea? It will only take a minute."

Jake leaned down and kissed his mother on the cheek. Although she was beginning to show her age, her skin was soft like a well-ripened peach. The once tiny lines at the corners of her eyes had deepened. With no makeup on, Jake could see the age spots that dotted her face.

"No thanks, Mom. We just came from eating dinner at Martini's. I'm as full as a tick on a lazy dog."

She laughed and gently patted him on the back.

Vicky hugged her mother-in-law and asked how she was doing.

"Oh, I'm doing quite well, Vicky. Thank you for asking. I'm not moving as fast as I used to, but I suppose that's to be expected. Y'all come into the den and have a seat. Are you sure I can't get you something? I have some fresh squeezed lemonade in the fridge."

"Nothing for me, Mama Tillery," answered Vicky.

"I'm fine too, Mom."

Before sitting down, Mrs. Tillery walked over to the TV and turned it off.

Jake and Vicky took a seat on the light-gold, French provincial sofa.

"I hope we're not disturbing your TV show," said Vicky.

Mrs. Tillery eased onto her recliner. "No, of course not. I can watch TV any old time. Visiting with my children is much more important than some old rerun of *The Andy Griffith Show* I've seen many times before. Now what is it you want to tell me? No wait…let me guess. You're pregnant."

Both Jake's and Vicky's mouth dropped open.

"How did you know, Mom?" Jake asked.

"Every pregnant woman I've ever known has a glow about her. And Vicky is glowing like a full moon in May. I noticed it at church last Sunday. This is the most wonderful news I could ever have hoped for. I'm finally going to be a grandmother. Your father would have been so happy."

"You are the first person we've told," said Jake.

Vicky quickly corrected him. "Well, not exactly the first, Jake. I say that because when I told Jake about us being pregnant, we were at the restaurant about to have dinner.

Once Jake got over the shock, he proceeded to shout it to every patron in the place."

Mrs. Tillery started laughing. "I bet he did at that. Do you know when it's due?"

"Not exactly," answered Vicky. "I'm thinking sometime in April."

"My birthday is in April. Maybe it will be born on the twentieth, then we can share birthdays. Have you told the Huberts yet?"

Jake reached over and touched his mother on the knee. "No, Mom. We wanted you to be the first in the family to know."

"That is so sweet, dear. I know they will be as excited as I am. You two have made my day. Better yet, you've made my year. I guess I'd better get busy crocheting some baby blankets. Oh, and I still have the cradle your father made for you when you were a baby. It's in the attic. It will need some cleaning done to it, but you're welcome to have it."

"Jake's old cradle would be perfect," said Vicky. "Jake can come get it down and clean it up as soon as we get the nursery ready."

"Don't be silly," said Mrs. Tillery. "He can get it down tonight, and I will work on cleaning it first thing in the morning."

"We don't want you to do that, Mom," said Jake. "I can clean it. You don't need to be doing strenuous work like that."

"Nonsense, Jake. I am perfectly capable of cleaning a cradle. Besides, what else do I have to do? It will be my pleasure. Now go get it down from the attic. I think it is near the front window beside your old rocking horse. We'll need to clean that up too, but for now, we'll just worry about the cradle."

Jake retreated to the attic while the two women talked. It had been years since he'd been in the attic. As he was searching for the cradle, he came across a box marked train set. *Wow*, he thought. *I'd forgotten all about this. Dad and I had some great times playing with that train.* He remembered how they used to lay down the tracks so it could run around the Christmas tree. Every year from the age of eight on up, Santa would add another boxcar to the set. Even after he was grown, the two of them would set it up on Christmas Eve and watch it go around and around the tree. Unfortunately, that tradition stopped when his dad died. It was a tradition he wanted to share with his child so he made a mental note to set up the train set the following Christmas.

Next to the train set was a box of toys. It was full of his favorite trucks, cars, and building blocks. They were covered in dust but still in decent shape. He picked up one of the trucks and rolled it across the floor. As he was doing so, a thought crossed his mind. *What if we have a girl? She won't want to play with trucks, cars, or even trains for that matter.* As quickly as the thought crossed his mind, he pushed it aside. As long as the baby was healthy, it didn't matter if it was a boy or a girl. He would love him or her just the same. After putting the truck back into the box, he spied the cradle exactly where his mother said it would be. It was covered with a thick piece of plastic and still had the mattress and pillow tucked inside.

When Jake returned to the den, Vicky seemed anxious. "What took you so long? Did you get lost?"

Jake sat the cradle on the coffee table in front of the sofa. "I found some of my old toys and my train set too."

"Oh, so you were playing with toys, huh?" Vicky teased.

"Yeah. There's some great stuff up there: Tonka trucks, cool race cars, Lincoln Logs, my rocking horse. He's gonna love that stuff when he's older."

"He?" asked Vicky. "What makes you think it's going to be a boy?"

"I'm just saying if it is a boy, he'll love that stuff."

Vicky ran her hand over the headboard of the cradle. "This is beautiful. Papa Tillery did a great job building this."

Mrs. Tillery spoke next. "He was very proud of that cradle. And in response to the baby being a boy or a girl. Jake, do you remember Alcyone Mullins? She was the little girl who lived next door to us when you were around ten."

Jake nodded, "Oh yeah, I remember her. Little red-haired girl with freckles and long pigtails."

"She liked playing with your trucks and cars almost as much as you did." Mrs. Tillery smiled.

"I wonder what ever happened to her," Jake pondered.

"I heard she joined the air force and got her degree in nursing," answered Mrs. Tillery. "I think she works at the hospital at Maxwell Air Force Base in Montgomery."

Jake shrugged his shoulders. "A nurse, huh? Who knew?"

Vicky slid to the edge of her chair. "Jake, I think we need to go. I'm sure it's past your mother's bedtime and I'm a little tired myself."

"No need to rush off on my account, dear," answered Mrs. Tillery. "I'm too excited about the baby to sleep. I have some phone calls to make. All these old fuddy-duddies who are always bragging about their grandchildren doing this and their grandchildren doing that. Well, now they'll have to listen to me brag for a change."

Jake kissed his mother on the cheek. "You're a trip, Mom, but I better get Vicky home. She needs her rest."

Mrs. Tillery stood up. "Thank you again for dropping by. I am so proud for both of you. A child is a wonderful gift you will enjoy the rest of your lives. Be safe going home. Love you both."

"Bye, Mom," said Vicky. "Let me know when you want us to pick up the cradle."

"I will. Have a good night you two."

When Jake arrived at work the next morning, he was so excited about the prospects of becoming a father he could hardly wait to tell everyone. The receptionist noticed right away he had something good going on.

"Good morning, Jake," she called to him as he entered the front door. "What are you so happy about?"

He stopped, leaned over her desk, and kissed her on the forehead. "Betty, I want you to send out a memo to all the staff requesting a meeting in the conference room at nine o'clock sharp. I have something very important to tell everyone. Can you do that for me?"

"Yes, of course, Jake," she replied. "Do you want to tell me what it is pertaining to?"

"You'll find out soon enough. Just send out the memo right away. Thanks."

As soon as Jake started down the hall toward his office, Betty began typing the request into her computer. Jake peeked in several doors along the way, speaking happily to whoever was on the other side. When he reached his office, Mrs. Peacock was sitting on one of the folding chairs just outside his door.

He immediately took her hand in his and kissed it. "Good morning, Mrs. Peacock," he said as he bowed in a most gentlemanly fashion.

Mrs. Peacock blushed. "I'm fine, Mr. Tillery. You look so happy. Are we finally getting married today?"

Jake moved in close and whispered something in her ear. Stepping back he said, "Now don't tell anyone. It's a secret. Okay."

Mrs. Peacock grinned. "Your secret is safe with me," she assured him.

"I have to go to a meeting in a few minutes, Mrs. Peacock. I won't be long. Would you like a cup of coffee or a glass of water while you wait?"

"No, Jake. I'm fine. I'll just wait here for you. The preacher should be here shortly. I brought along a travel magazine to look at. I'll be deciding where I want to go on our honeymoon."

"That's a very good idea. I'll be back shortly, and you can tell me all about it."

Jake went into his office and placed the stack of files back on his desk. He had intended on reading them the night before, but that never happened. He and Vicky had spent much of the night talking and making plans for the new arrival. They had even picked out names. Linda Cynan if it was a girl and Dawson Arlen if it was a boy. Jake glanced at the clock. It was five minutes until nine. The phone was ringing, but he decided it would have to wait until after the meeting.

The conference room was filling up quickly as other case workers and their aides filed in, curious as to what was going on. When everyone was present, Jake stepped forward.

"First, let me say thank you for taking time out of your busy day to come to this meeting on such short notice. I know everyone has a full load today, so I will get right to the point. Vicky and I are going to have a baby."

Everyone who had worked at Social Services for any length of time knew how hard and how long Jake and

Vicky had tried so desperately to get pregnant. The room erupted in applause and congratulations. The men came forward to shake Jake's hand. The women gave him hugs along with tears and sniffles. When everyone had their turn at congratulating him, they returned to their duties leaving Jake alone, staring out the window. As he was staring, he noticed a redbird sitting on a tree limb just outside the window. She had a twig in her mouth. As he was watching, the redbird hopped over to the nest she was building. Carefully, she placed the twig in her nest and moved it around until she was satisfied in its placement. Soon, there appeared a male redbird. His bright red feathers made a much more beautiful specimen than his mate. He too had a small twig in his mouth. However, instead of placing the twig in the nest himself, he handed it off to the female, leaving her to fasten it into the nest while he went in search of another piece of building material.

The redbirds building their nest brought him to mind of the nursery he and Vicky would soon be preparing for the new baby. Much like the birds outside the window, he would bring the twigs and Vicky would build the nest to her liking. A new generation; the ebb and flow of life.

The coming weekend, Jake and Vicky made an unexpected visit to Montgomery, to the house Dawson shared with his mother, Mama Cora, as she was known by her family. They arrived just after eight to find Beth and Kayleen already there. When they approached the front door, Jake could hear Kayleen talking to her mother about wanting to go on a triple date with her friends: Cindy and Joe, Cheri and Mike, and of course, her latest boyfriend, Daniel. It was obvious neither Beth nor Dawson were happy about the prospects.

"I think we should rescue Kayleen," joked Jake. "What do you think?"

Vicky smiled. "I don't know if we would be rescuing Kayleen or rescuing Beth and Dawson."

Jake opened the door and called out to them, "Anybody home?"

Kayleen was the first to jump up from the table. As she was headed toward the door, she yelled to the rest of the family, "It's Uncle Jake and Aunt Vicky!" She hugged Jake first and then Vicky. "Why didn't you tell us you were coming? It's so good to see you."

Jake could see the rest of the family getting up from the table and called out to them, "Don't let us disturb your breakfast. Keep eating. We'll come to you."

Jake, Vicky, and Kayleen made their way to the dining area. "Something sure smells good in here," said Vicky.

Mama Cora hugged both Vicky's and Jake's neck and ordered them both to have a seat at the table. "How do the two of ya' like your eggs?"

"None for me, Mama Cora," replied Jake. "But I will have one of your biscuits and some syrup and butter to sop."

Dawson smiled. "Hard to beat Mama's homemade biscuits."

"I'll just have a bowl of grits," answered Vicky. "And maybe a couple of pieces of bacon…Hmm, I don't know, maybe a biscuit or two. And do you still have some of that blueberry jam you made last summer?"

Mama Cora looked surprised. She'd never known Vicky to eat much at one time. She always said she had to watch her weight. "I'm glad to see you eatin' better, Vicky."

Jake and Vicky looked at one another and smiled.

"That's kinda why we're here, Mama Cora," said Jake. "You see, Vicky is eating for two now."

Mama Cora almost dropped the jar of blueberry jam she'd taken out of the refrigerator. "Eatin' for two!" she exclaimed. "Are y'all havin' a baby?"

Jake and Vicky grinned like a honeybee in a field full of clover and nodded yes.

Mama Cora threw up her hands. "Well, glory be and praise the Lord! Ain't that somethin'. Did ya hear that, Dawson? You're gonna be another granddaddy and Beth's gonna be an aunt."

Kayleen quickly jumped in with her two cents' worth. "And I'm gonna have a little cousin!"

Everyone was so excited they almost forgot to finish eating their breakfast. Everyone except Vicky that is. After all, she was eating for two and both of them were starving.

The following Monday morning passed quickly for Jake. After lunch, he returned to find an unfamiliar face sitting in one of the chairs outside his door. He was wearing a hat pulled low across his forehead. His chin was resting on his chest as though he was asleep. Jake touched him on the shoulder to awaken him. Startled, the man jumped up; his hands balled up into fists, ready to defend himself. Jake took several steps back.

"Calm down, sir. I'm sorry I frightened you. I'm Jake Tillery. And you are?"

The slight-built man dropped his hands, but they remained tight fisted at his side. "I'm Judas Solomon. I was told by my parole officer, Tom Denny, to come here today. Somethin' 'bout gettin' food stamps, money, and a place to live."

Jake looked at Judas curiously. So this was the man Mrs. Porter had assigned to him. He didn't necessarily look like a murderer, but then again, what was a killer supposed to look like?

"Come into my office, Mr. Solomon. I will need to get some information from you in order to get things underway."

Judas followed Jake into his office. Jake pointed to the chair opposite his. "Have a seat, Mr. Solomon."

"I'd rather ya' call me Judas. Ain't nobody ever called me Mr. Solomon 'cept the warden. Didn't like him, and I don't like bein' called Mr. Solomon."

Jake was not comfortable calling him by his first name. First names were personal, and the last thing Jake wanted was to be personal with Judas Solomon, especially after what he'd read about him. Still, if he preferred to be called by his first name, he would try to oblige.

"Fine, Judas. Please…have a seat."

Judas slumped down onto the straight-backed chair. "Ain't very comfortable, is it?"

"What's that, Judas?"

"The chair. It ain't very comfortable."

Jake had really never thought about whether the chair was comfortable or not, and in Judas's case, he really didn't care. He didn't think being murdered was very comfortable for the young woman Judas had killed.

"I suppose not," Jake responded rather curtly. "So, Judas, where are you living now?"

Judas rubbed at a spot on the leg of his brown trousers that appeared to be a grease stain.

"One of them halfway houses over on Sixteenth Avenue," he replied.

"That would be the Baldwin House."

"I reckon that's what they call it."

"It says here you have no immediate family. Is that correct?"

"None that'll have anything to do with me."

I can understand why, Jake thought.

"How old are you?"

Judas thought for a minute. "I reckon I'm somewhere round sixty-five. I ain't real shore. My mama had me at home, then just took off. My daddy raised me and my two stepbrothers. He was mean to us boys. I hated his guts. He got drunk one night when I was around ten or 'leven. Clyde was the youngest, maybe three or four. Young'un wasn't doin' nothin', just makin' a little noise with the truck he was playin' with. All of a sudden, Daddy pulled off his belt and went to beatin' on Clyde. Well, I'd done had enough of that old man actin' like some kinda fool. I picked up a baseball bat and hit him on the head. Bashed his head in flatter than a flitter. After that, we was all sent to the orphanage. Clyde and Leonard got adopted out. I run away and never went back. Lived on my own after that."

For the moment, Jake sat staring at Judas. In his mind, he wondered how his own life might have been different had he not spent it in a good home with parents who loved and protected him. In a way, he felt sorry for Judas. Still, he'd known people who came from worse situations who turned out to be good people and good citizens.

When Judas noticed Jake staring at him, his passive demeanor quickly changed.

"Why ya lookin' at me like that?" he roared.

Jake immediately looked away. "Sorry," he replied. "I talked to the lady at Belview Apartments. She will have an opening for a two-room apartment the first of next month. Until then, you can stay at the Baldwin House. You will be issued a Medicaid card at the front desk with a list of participating doctors."

"When do I start gettin' money?" asked Judas.

"It will take a month or so before your monthly checks will start. Out of those checks you will be paying twenty dollars a month as partial payment for your rent. The state will be responsible for the remainder of the cost. Until then, you will be given twenty-five dollars every two weeks for necessities."

Judas lurched forward making Jake flinch. "Twenty-five dollars!" he yelled. "Is that all? I can spend that much on food and cigarettes in a couple of days."

The nerve of this guy, thought Jake. Without hesitation, Jake fired back, "The taxpayers of this state are not responsible for buying your cigarettes, Mr. Solomon."

Judas quickly rose to his feet, leaned across the desk, and slammed his fist down hard, rattling the picture of Vicky and almost making it topple over.

"I told ya' I hate bein' called Mr. Solomon!"

Jake was not intimidated by Judas.

"Sit down, Mr. Solomon!" he shouted firmly. "Don't make me have to call security."

Judas reluctantly eased back onto his chair.

"One more outburst like that in my office and you will be finishing out your prison sentence behind bars. Is that understood…Mr. Solomon?"

Judas dropped his head and nodded yes. Yet Jake could see him sneering and feel him seething under his breath. *Why does the parole board let prisoners like Judas Solomon out of prison in the first place?* he thought. *It is obvious this man is a danger to society.* Jake leaned back in his chair and continued on with his instructions.

"As I was saying, Mr. Solomon, although you have been released from prison, you will still be monitored by both me and Mr. Denny. If you do not show up for your appointments with either of us, you will be sent back to prison. If you cause a disturbance either in the halfway house or the apartment you will be assigned to, you will be sent back to prison. If you are found with a weapon, you will be sent back to prison. You are not allowed to leave the state unless you are given permission by either me or Mr. Denny. If you do—"

Judas blatantly interrupted Jake, "I'll be sent back to prison."

Jake leaned forward, laid his paperwork on his desk, and glared at Judas. After several moments of silence, he spoke, "Your attitude is less than hospitable, Mr. Solomon. And to be honest with you, I don't like you or your attitude. Rest assured, Judas, I will be keeping a close watch on you. It would be in your best interest to adjust your smart-mouthed attitude and work on doing your best to live by the rules I have laid out for you."

Judas did not look at Jake nor did he seem intimidated by the rules and regulations of his parole. He simply continued mumbling something under his breath.

"I can see already you're going to end up doing time again unless you straighten up and fly right," Jake concluded.

This time Judas stared at Jake harshly. "Can I go now, Mr. Tillery?" he asked indignantly.

Jake hesitated. "Yes, Mr. Solomon. You can go now. I will see you again two weeks from today. Is that clear?"

Judas rose to his feet and picked up the picture from off Jake's desk. "Is this your old lady?"

Jake reached for the photograph of Vicky, took it from Judas, and placed it back on his desk. "Yes, that is my wife," he answered.

Judas smiled a crooked grin. "Pretty lady. Bet she's good in bed too. Huh, Mr. Tillery?"

Jake could feel himself losing control. Something he rarely ever did. "Good-bye, Mr. Solomon!" he said sternly.

Judas turned and headed for the door. As he reached for the doorknob, he turned toward Jake. "Tell your old lady I said hello," he jeered.

Before Jake could respond, Judas was out the door. As he was leaving, he met Mrs. Peacock in the hallway. She was dressed in her pretty pink dress and blue sunhat. As he passed, he reached out, touched her aging breast, and hauntingly laughed at the surprised look on her face. She immediately pulled away and began to cry. Judas, without remorse, casually walked to the exit, leaving poor Mrs. Peacock in shock. When she entered Jake's office, he inquired as to why she was crying. She was too humiliated and embarrassed to tell him about what Judas had done, so she lied and said she stubbed her toe on the door facing on her way in.

3

An Important Find

The months were passing quickly. Vicky was in her sixth month. Jake joked with her, saying she looked as though she'd swallowed a basketball. She would answer back by saying she felt like she had swallowed two basketballs. The nursery was coming along nicely too. Since they didn't know the gender of the baby, they had decided to decorate it in yellow and green rather than pink or blue. The walls were painted a light green. Jake put wallpaper on one wall with a matching border of puppies and kittens sitting in yellow baskets around the top of the other three walls.

Jake's mother had cleaned Jake's old cradle to look as good as new. She even painted a kitten cuddled up in the arms of a puppy on the head of the cradle to match the wallpaper. There was a white baby bed with sheets and a pillow that also matched the puppy and kitten theme. Above the bed hung a mobile of kittens and puppies. With the flip of a switch, the mobile would begin turning and playing "How Much Is That Doggie in the Window."

As Jake and Vicky stood back admiring their achievements, Jake commented on their work, "I sure hope our kid likes puppies and kittens."

Vicky laughed. "If he or she doesn't, we're in trouble."

Since both of them had worked all the years they had been married, they had managed to save a substantial amount of money. It was decided Vicky would continue working until the baby came. Afterward, she would become a stay-at-home mom as neither of them wanted to leave raising their child to a babysitter or daycare worker.

Jake had recently gotten a promotion at work and was now a supervisor. He only saw clients when the social workers under him were sick or on vacation. When he was promoted to supervisor, they hired another social worker to take Jake's place. Her name was Lyndsay Cannon. She was twenty-four years old, newly married, and only recently graduated from college. She was petite and rather shy. Jake worried she might have trouble dealing with people like Judas Solomon. However, despite Jake's objection, Mrs. Porter, who had been promoted to manager over the entire agency, insisted Lyndsay be given all of Jake's old clientele, including Judas Solomon.

When Jake was turning over the files, he made sure he informed Lyndsay all he knew about Judas Solomon. "He can be a difficult person to deal with," he told her. "Don't let him intimidate you, and if he gives you too much trouble, let me know and I will handle him personally, regardless of what Mrs. Porter has to say. It will be between the two of us. Understand?"

Lyndsay appreciated Jake's concern but assured him she felt she could handle Mr. Solomon without too much difficulty. Jake wasn't so sure, especially after Lyndsay came in sick to her stomach three days in a row. He'd seen this same reaction after Vicky found out she was pregnant. She would eat, be sick, then eat some more, only to be sick again. On the third morning after she'd showed signs of morning sickness, Jake came right out and asked her.

"Lyndsay, are you by any chance pregnant?"

Immediately, she began to cry, another sure sign that he was right.

"Now don't cry, Lyndsay. Everything will be okay." He tried his best to console her. "There's nothing to get upset about."

"But, Mr. Tillery," she cried.

"Please, Lyndsay, call me Jake."

"Yes sir, Mr. Tillery. I mean, Jake. As you know, I just got married a year ago. We weren't planning on having children right away. Terry just started his new job at the brokerage firm, and I just got started here. Please don't fire me. I promise I'll work hard, and I'll work right up until time for the baby to come. My mother can take care of the baby, and I'll get back to work as soon as I get out of the hospital."

Jake smiled at her optimism. "That won't be necessary. You are guaranteed six weeks paid leave after having a baby.

Your job will be here when you get back. At least if I have anything to say about it. Now don't cry anymore. Okay?"

"Yes sir, Mr. Tillery. I mean, Jake."

"Fine. By the way, I've been wanting to ask you how it's going with Judas Solomon. Is he giving you any grief?"

"No. Actually, he's been very nice to me. He always asks me about my family and how my house decorating is coming. It seems as though he's made a real turnaround."

Jake immediately became concerned. "Listen, Lyndsay, I don't want to alarm you, but you never want to give out any personal information to your clients, especially ones with criminal backgrounds."

Lyndsay smiled. "I really don't think I have anything to worry about with Mr. Solomon. He's been nothing but hospitable and sincere in his dealings with me."

"That's good. I hope it stays that way, Lyndsay. But if it doesn't, you let me know right away."

"I will. I promise."

Vicky arrived home around five in the afternoon. The channel 6 evening news was about to start. Although she worked for one of the biggest newspapers in Alabama, she always wanted to make sure every big story was covered. She hurriedly put her purse on the table just inside the door and turned on the TV. Across the screen flashed an alert,

Breaking News. Vicky sat down on the sofa and turned up the volume.

"Good evening," the newscaster, Jeannie Graham, said soberly. "FOX6 News reporter, Stacey Furguson, is standing by with breaking news from Trussville where a body has been discovered in an abandoned house. Stacey."

The camera switched over to a pretty blonde girl standing in front of a house that had obviously been neglected for a long period of time. The grass and tall weeds had taken over the yard. There were beer cans, empty liquor bottles, and food wrappers strewn around the perimeter of the dilapidated porch. Heavy, sun-bleached curtains and what appeared to be ragged, dirty bed sheets hung haphazardly at the windows. Some of the window panes were completely missing, the glass lying broken and scattered on the ground beneath the window.

"I am standing in front of the house where, earlier this afternoon, a body was discovered. Police reported the body was that of a black female in her mid to late twenties. It was obvious to the officers, who are investigating the crime, she had been beaten to death with a blunt object. Detective Jim Crawford, a homicide investigator for the Trussville Police Department, said the unidentified female had apparently been dead for several days. Her body has been removed by the coroner's office, and the detectives are awaiting positive identification. Nothing more is known about this case as of now. Back to you, Jeannie."

Vicky turned off the TV and immediately called her editor. After two rings, he answered, "Birmingham News, this is Fred Swenson."

"Fred, this is Vicky. Have you heard about the woman's body they found over in Trussville?"

"Yes, Vick. I sent Brandon Lockhart over there to check it out."

Vicky made a huffing sound. "Brandon Lockhart! Fred, why didn't you assign this one to me? You know Brandon never asks enough questions. And he leaves out half the story."

"I know that, Vick, but I didn't think you needed to be handling a story like this in the condition you're in."

Disgusted that she didn't get the story, Vicky placed her hand on her hip. Although Fred could not see her, he'd known Vicky long enough to know her reaction.

"Do you mean because I'm pregnant? Is that really why I didn't get it?"

"Yes, Vick. That's exactly why. It is my understanding the victim was also possibly pregnant. Besides, that address is a known drug house. She was probably killed over some drug deal. No big news there."

"Well, I still think I should have gotten the story. I'm a good reporter. Just because I'm pregnant doesn't mean I can't write a report about a murder."

"You're right, Vick. You are a good reporter. Without a doubt, you're the best reporter I have on staff. I'm just trying to look out for you. You've waited a long time to have a baby, and I don't want anything to mess it up for you. So let's leave the gruesome murder cases to someone else for the time being. Okay?"

"Fine! But I still say I could have done a better job of reporting the crime than Brandon."

Fred smiled and said his good-byes.

Vicky was just hanging up the phone when Jake came through the front door.

"Vick," he called out, "I'm home."

Vicky walked into the foyer. Jake was hanging his jacket on the coatrack. "How was your day?" he asked.

"Fine, but I'm angry with Fred."

"What did poor Fred do now?"

"I just found out that he gave a lead story to Brandon Lockhart instead of me."

Jake kissed her on the cheek. "And what lead story would that be?"

"They found a woman's body in an abandoned house over in Trussville. She was obviously beaten to death."

"Well, frankly, Vick, I'm glad he gave a story like that to another reporter. You don't need to be seeing dead bodies in your condition."

"That's what Fred said."

Jake put his arm around Vicky's shoulder and headed her toward the kitchen. "Smart man that Fred. What would you like for supper?"

"I forgot to put anything out this morning," Vicky answered. "But we do have some leftover meatloaf. We could make a couple of meatloaf sandwiches with potato chips and one of the kosher dill pickles Mama Cora made. They are so good. I wish I had the time to make homemade pickles like she does. I could eat a whole jar in one sitting."

"Is that you or the baby talking?" Jake laughed.

The next morning was Saturday. Jake rose early, put the coffee on, and went out front to get the paper. It was a beautiful morning, cool and crisp. The sun was shining, the birds were singing, and the hummingbirds were making mad dashes at the feeder hanging on the pole near the white picket fence. Jake liked watching the hummingbirds—the way their wings fluttered so fast you could barely see them moving. At times they would get angry with one another. One would chase the other away from the feeder. Jake stood on the stoop watching them until he heard the beeper go off on the coffeemaker letting him know the cycle was finished and the coffee was ready.

When he was finished filling his coffee mug, he turned to see Vicky standing in the doorway. Her hair was disheveled, and Jake could have sworn her belly had grown two sizes bigger overnight. He smiled, walked over to her, and kissed her on the forehead.

"How is my little sleepy head this morning?"

"I need coffee," she answered pitifully.

Jake led her over to the breakfast nook and helped her get seated. "I'll get my little dumpling a cup of coffee. You just sit here and relax," he said in a babyish tone.

While Jake was getting Vicky's coffee, she reached for the morning paper Jake had laid on the table. Opening it, she began looking for the article about the slain woman they'd found in the abandoned house. To her surprise, it was not on the front page. Flipping through the pages, she located a small one-column article on page three titled, "Woman Found Slain in Trussville."

"I can't believe this!" she shouted.

Concerned, Jake quickly turned to see what she was so upset about. "You can't believe what, honey?"

"I tried to tell Fred he should have given me the story. This piddly little article Brandon wrote isn't even worth publishing."

Jake sat Vicky's mug on the table in front of her. "And what story would that be?"

"The one I was telling you about last night. The one about the woman they found killed over in Trussville. Just look at this."

She shoved the paper toward Jake. "I guarantee you, had it been one of the Birmingham socialites that was murdered, it would have made front page."

Jake spoke calmly so as to try and restore tranquility to the conversation. He didn't like Vicky getting upset in her fragile condition. "Now, Vicky honey, you know that's how it is and always has been. As I said earlier, she was probably involved in a drug deal gone bad. The police department probably asked Fred to play it down so as not to alarm the public."

"Still, even if it was a drug deal, even if she was a prostitute, her story deserves to be told, not stuck on page three at the bottom of the page."

"Well, honey, that's not your decision now, is it?"

"No, but you can bet if it had been my decision, the story would be on the front page."

"Do they know her identity yet?"

"Who knows! Even if they did, Brandon is too dumb to find out. The only thing he's good for, as far as being a reporter is concerned, is giving the scores to the football games on Friday night. Even at that, he can't write a decent account of the important plays made in the games. He does write down the scores when they're called in and sometimes even those aren't correct."

Jake decided it was time to change the subject. "What do you want to do today?"

"I'd like to fire Brandon."

Jake laughed. "Besides firing Brandon?"

"I'd like to take a look at the house where they found the dead woman's body."

Jake finished his coffee and was ready for his second cup. He stood up and started toward the pot. "Are you ready for another cup?"

"No thanks. I'm trying to keep my caffeine drinking down to a minimal. My OBGYN said it would be better for the baby."

Jake filled his cup. "Vicky, are you sure you want to spend your day off looking at a bloody crime scene?"

"Yes, I do. There's something about this case. I don't know what it is. I guess you can call it a reporter's instinct, a woman's intuition, or just a gut feeling, but I need to do this."

"Then that's what we'll do. After all, you followed me halfway around Montgomery looking for someone we weren't even sure existed."

"Yeah, and look where that got us."

Jake took a sip of his coffee and smiled. "A family I never knew I had."

After breakfast, Jake and Vicky got dressed and set out for Trussville. By the time they arrived at the crime scene, it was around ten in the morning. A yellow crime tape surrounded the entire yard. "How are we going to get past the yellow crime scene tape?" asked Jake.

"If we're lucky, one of the guys I know from the police station will be keeping watch and will let me in."

"And if one of the guys you know from the police station isn't on duty keeping watch, what do you plan to do to get in?"

Vicky got out of the car with Jake close behind. They walked to the edge of the yard and Vicky called out, "Helloooo. Anybody here?"

"There appears to be no one here, so I guess we'll be leaving now," said Jake, somewhat relieved.

"Hellooo," Vicky called louder. "It's Vicky Tillery, a reporter from the Birmingham News. Is it okay if we come in and take a look around?"

No one answered.

"Remember when you asked me what we would do if no one from the police department was here to let us in?"

"Yes."

Vicky lifted the tape and stepped under it. "This is what we do."

Jake hesitated. "Ahhh, Vick, really now, should we be doing this? I mean, I'm thinking this crime scene tape is here for a reason. Say, to keep people from entering the crime scene."

"We'll be in and out without anyone ever knowing. Come on. Just act like you know what you're doing."

"What are we doing?"

"We're investigating a murder, Jake. Isn't it exciting?"

Vicky started across the yard with Jake close behind.

"Honestly, Vick. This is not my kind of excitement."

The front door was not locked nor was there any evidence of an attempt to keep anyone from entering. "You see," said Vicky, "chances are the police won't even come back. Otherwise, they would have secured the door."

Vicky pushed open the door and started to go inside. Jake placed his hand on her arm to stop her.

"Wait, Vick. Let me go first, just in case there is someone here."

Vicky smiled at his gallantry. "Okay, you go first if it'll make you feel better."

"Well, it won't necessarily make me feel better, but being I am a man, it seems reasonable that it would be the right thing to do."

Jake stepped inside and Vicky followed. Although it was daylight, the room was dark. In the first room, heavy, tattered, crimson curtains covered the windows blocking most of the sunlight. As their eyes adjusted to the darkness, they were able to see that the living room was bare of furnishings. Except for an abundance of empty beer cans, some hamburger wrappers, as well as an array of used hypodermic needles, there was little else. To the right was what appeared to be a kitchen. A small metal table was covered in discarded boxes that once had held fried chicken. Only the stench of rotting bones remained. They crossed the room and into the hallway. To the left of the hall was a bedroom and next to it was a bathroom. There were no curtains on the windows, making it somewhat easier to see.

Vicky pushed open the bathroom door. The commode was filled with human waste.

Vicky covered her nose. "Gross," she said as she pinched her nostrils shut with her thumb and index finger.

Venturing further down the hall, they came to a second bedroom. There on the floor was a chalk drawing of where the victim's body had once lain. Jake and Vicky stepped carefully so they wouldn't step in the pool of dried blood on the floor.

"This must be where they found her," said Jake.

Vicky pulled a small flashlight from her purse and turned it on. "I almost forgot I had this." She pointed the beam toward the walls. Blood splatters covered all four walls. A filthy urine and semen covered mattress was lying in one corner. It was also bloody. Hand prints on the floor looked as though the victim had tried to pull herself to safety.

"I would say she put up a fight," Jake reasoned.

"There is so much blood. He must have beaten her severely. Look over there."

Vicky pointed to what appeared to be small piece of intestine next to the mattress. "Is that what I think it is?"

"Well, if you're thinking it looks like guts, then I think you're thinking right."

"That's disgusting."

"Are you ready to leave now?" Jake asked, not as a question, but as a conclusion.

"Not yet," answered Vicky. "Let's take a look outside."

The stench was almost unbearable. "Anything to get out of this house," Jake agreed.

Jake and Vicky made their way down the hall and toward the kitchen door. To get to the back door, they had to go through the kitchen. The sink was filled with stagnate water. Unidentifiable objects lay on top of the water and were covered in a grayish mold. The skeletal remains of a dead mouse lay next to the sink. Roaches, both dead and alive, were everywhere you looked. Vicky hated roaches. When one of the long, brown, hard-shelled creatures ran across the toe of her shoe, she was more than happy to get out of the house as rapidly as possible.

When Jake opened the back door, he saw that the screen door was hanging halfway on and halfway off its hinges. He pushed the screen door away from the door frame so Vicky could get past it. The half rotten steps were the next obstacle. He reached and took her hand.

"Be careful going down these steps, Vick. They don't look too safe," he warned her.

Once they were out back, they saw a rickety aluminum shed. The door was hanging on by a single rusty bolt.

"Let's take a look inside it," Vicky suggested.

"Probably just junk," Jake replied. "But we'll look if it makes you happy."

Jake pulled back the hanging door as much as possible. Vicky pointed her flashlight inside. To their surprise, were the remains of what appeared to be a meth lab.

"Oh my goodness!" Vicky shouted. "Can you believe this? It's a wonder whoever was living here wasn't blown to bits."

"Can we go now, Vick? You don't need to be around all this in your condition."

"Yes, honey," Vicky answered, amused by Jake's concern. "I've seen enough. The next step is to see if the police have identified the victim and if they have any suspects."

As they were walking around the side of the house, Jake noticed something protruding outward from the crawlspace. It looked like the end of a wooden handle. He started to reach for it, but Vicky stopped him.

"Wait, Jake," she warned. "That might be evidence. Use you handkerchief to pick it up."

Jake took out his handkerchief and placed it over the handle. As Jake pulled it from its hiding place, it became apparent that it was indeed a possible piece of evidence as it was covered in blood. The object was a hatchet; much like what a boy scout would use on a camping trip.

"I don't know how the investigators missed this," Jake said.

"I told you, Jake. When the victim is a known drug abuser, a prostitute, or a homeless person, the police do little to solve the crime. They figure the murder is drug related or has something to do with an unhappy client of a call girl."

"So now what do we do?"

"We take this hatchet to the police station and turn it over to the detectives as evidence."

Jake thought for a moment. "And how do we explain what we were doing, poking around one of their crime scenes? Besides, if there is evidence on the handle, a defense lawyer could argue that we didn't have a search warrant so the evidence was obtained illegally. The judge might throw it out, and the killer would get away with murder."

Vicky looked puzzled. "How do you know about search warrants and illegal searches?"

"Hey, I do watch TV you know: *Father Dowling Mysteries*, *21 Jump Street*, and *America's Most Wanted*, just to name a few."

Vicky decided they should put the hatchet back where they had found it. "Okay, perhaps you're right."

Jake abruptly stopped her. "I'm right! Did I hear you say I'm right?" he joked.

Vicky smiled. "I have to give you a little credit. You are occasionally right about a few things. We'll go see my detective friend at the police station and tell him about what we found. So put the hatchet back just like we found it."

Jake placed the hatchet back in the crawlspace. As soon as they were back in the car, Jake drove to the police station. When they went inside, several officers standing around the station waved and spoke to her. She called one of the officers by name and asked how his wife and new baby were doing. He told her they were both doing well. He also asked how her pregnancy was progressing.

Jake was surprised that Vicky knew these officers on a first-name basis. He knew she'd been a reporter with the Birmingham News for almost twenty years, but he'd never thought about how she could also be involved with the police department. However, once he considered it, it would seem only reasonable. The desk sergeant greeted her with the same friendly attitude as the officer.

"Hi there, Vicky. What are you doing here today?"

She told him she needed to see Detective Jim Crawford.

The desk sergeant tilted his head downward and looked over the top of his reading glasses. "He's in his office. Just go on back. You know where it is."

There were desks and chairs everywhere you looked. Phones were ringing constantly. Men dressed in suits with their ties loosened sat at their desks, asking questions and taking notes of potential suspects. Many of the suspects were in handcuffs. Some looked like they belonged in custody, while others looked like normal everyday people you would meet on the street.

As Vicky and Jake made their way through the maze of desks, Jake wondered what had happened to these people that made them break the law. Had they been raised without parents or by parents who didn't care about their well-being? Were they a victim of child abuse or worse, sexual abuse? As a social worker, Jake knew there were people from all walks of life, and for many of them, the way they turned out was no real fault of their own. That was why he became a social worker in the first place—to help those less fortunate become pillars of the community. It certainly wasn't for the money. Social workers were one of the lowest paying positions on the totem pole.

When Jake and Vicky finally reached the more private offices, she stopped at the first door on the right and knocked. The offices were made of glass from three feet upward. Jake could see a rather robust gentleman in his mid to late fifties sitting at his desk. A stack of files a foot high reminded Jake of his own desk. When the man looked up, he smiled and motioned them to enter. As they entered, the man got to his feet and welcomed them in.

"Hello, Miss Vicky, and how are you today?" he asked joyfully.

"I am fine, Jim. How are you?"

"I've had better days, but I can't complain," he answered jokingly. "And who is this fellow with you?"

Jake put forth his hand, and Jim gladly shook it.

"This is my husband, Jake. Jake, Detective Jim Crawford."

"Call me Jim. Everybody else does," he said to Jake as he pointed to the chairs in front of his desk.

"Glad to meet you, Jim," Jake replied, taking the chair next to Vicky, who had already seated herself.

Jim sat down and looked at Vicky. "And what information might Birmingham's ace reporter be interested in today?"

"Well, Jim," Vicky began. "Jake and I went to the house where the young woman was killed. The one over in Trussville."

"Yes, I know the one you're referring to. But I thought they gave that story to that Brandon fellow."

"Yes, they did, and I read his article in this morning's paper. My fifteen-year-old niece could have done a better job."

"Now, Vicky," Jim said jokingly, "give the boy a break. Not everyone is an ace reporter like yourself."

Vicky shifted slightly in her chair. Her urge to urinate, due to the baby putting pressure on her bladder, was becoming more frequent.

"Yeah, well, I suppose you're right," she agreed. "Still, if you ask me, he did a poor job of reporting the young woman's death."

Jim reared back in his chair; his hands locked together behind his head. His massive stomach bulged outward over his pants, hiding the black belt holding them up.

"So, Vicky, am I to assume this visit has something to do with the Trussville murder?" he asked.

"Yes, Jim, it does. You see, Jake and I went there this morning to look around and—"

At that point, Jim interrupted her statement. "And I don't suppose the crime tape, which clearly states not to cross, made any difference?"

Jake squirmed in his seat, but Vicky went forward as if he had said nothing.

"Anyway, we didn't find anything inside the house. However, while we were looking around outside, we came across a bloody hatchet that appeared to have been thrown under the house at the opening of the crawl space. I'm really quite surprised your officers didn't find it."

Jim unlocked his hands and leaned forward, placing his elbows on his desk. "I see. And what did you do with the hatchet, may I ask?"

"We left it there, of course," answered Vicky. "I wanted to bring it to you, but Jake pointed out that it might be better if the police found and removed it instead."

Jim looked at Jake and smiled. "I like your husband's thinking, Vicky."

Once Vicky told Jim about the hatchet, she was ready for him to give her any information that she might need to write a better story than that of Brandon's.

"So tell me, Jim. Have you any suspects? Has the coroner determined the time of death? How was she killed? Have you identified her?"

Jim threw up his hands. "Whoa, girl. One question at a time. No, we do not have any suspects. I figure it to be drug related. She had track marks on both arms. The coroner said her time of death appeared to have been several days ago. The body had already begun to decompose, and the rodents had consumed parts of her. At this time, it is hard to say the cause of death. However, I will tell you that the hatchet you and Jake found under the house could very well be the instrument used to kill her. We have not identified her. She had nothing on her that would tell us who she is: no driver's license, no ID of any kind. We may never be able to identify her unless someone comes forward with a missing person's report or if by chance she has a police record. Even then, I'm not sure if we will be able to identify her. As I said before, rats and who knows what else had already begun consuming her body."

While Vicky was busy writing notes, Jake made a statement of his own. "Sounds like you're saying this will be one of those unfortunate murders that never gets solved."

Jim looked solemn. "That's about right. This type of murder happens quite often in the area where she was found. Many of them are never solved. When there are witnesses, they're afraid to speak up for fear of retaliation. It's a never-ending thing: gang violence, drug dealers, murders, robberies, assaults, prostitutes as young as twelve years old. It never ends."

Jake dropped his head. "I see a lot of the results stemming from all you've said. I'm a social worker. We often get the leftovers of these violent acts."

Jim nodded and turned his attention to Vicky. "Vicky, I know you're a terrific reporter. You're one of the best. But I really wish you'd steer clear of these kinds of stories.

You've got more to think about now than just yourself." He pointed to her ever-expanding waistline.

Jake agreed, "I keep telling her the same thing."

Vicky stopped writing and touched her stomach. "I know you're both right, but it's hard not to cover a story like this. You know yourself, Jim. If it were some big socialite that was murdered, it would make front page news no matter who wrote it. But let a murder happen on the so-called 'wrong side of town,' and it barely gets mentioned. I feel like I have to be a voice for these women. After all, they're someone's daughter, someone's mother, someone's sister. Who's going to speak out for them? Certainly not Brandon Lockhart."

Jim raised his eyebrows. "I suppose you're right, little lady. Just promise me you'll be careful. I would hate to see something bad happen to you."

"Tell her about it," Jake agreed.

Vicky looked at one, then the other. "I hear you both, and I promise I will be careful. However, right now, my bladder is telling me I need to find the john. If you will excuse me, I'll be back shortly."

Vicky rose and quickly headed out the door toward the restrooms. Jake and Jim remained seated.

Jim watched as Vicky hurried down the hallway and into the female employee bathroom. He then turned his attention to Jake.

"I know you know your wife better than anyone else. And you know once she sets her mind on something, she rarely lets it go."

Jake nodded his head in agreement.

"Whoever did this particular murder is extremely violent. That poor girl was not only beaten, she was chopped to pieces. Probably with the same hatchet the two of you discovered at the scene. I'm just saying, keep a close watch on Vicky. She's a great lady. I'd hate to see anything happen to her."

"Do you have any leads at all, Detective?"

"There was nothing at the scene that could tie any one person to the crime. We found dozens of prints, several different blood types and semen, but with all the traffic passing through there, there's no way to tell who the possible killer or killers are. Hopefully, the hatchet will give us a more substantial lead. To tell you the truth, I don't know how my men missed it."

"In all honesty, Detective, I can see how it could have easily been overlooked. It was pure luck that I saw it."

Moments later, Vicky returned from her restroom break. "Sorry about that, fellows. Nowadays, when nature calls, it must be answered. Did I miss anything?"

"Only the biggest story to hit Birmingham in over forty years," Jim answered jokingly.

Vicky snickered, "Right."

They all had a good laugh.

Jim got to his feet and reached across his desk to give Vicky and Jake a good-bye handshake. "I want to thank the two of you for your help. My partner and I will head over there right away and get the hatchet. I'll let you know if we turn up anything further."

Jake and Vicky said their good-byes. Before walking out of the office, Vicky turned to Jim. "By the way, who are you partnering with since Joe Garrard retired?"

"A young rookie by the name of Andy Boone. Green as a gourd, but he's coming along. I would introduce him to you, but he isn't here. I sent him to get some donuts. Everybody in the precinct ordered something different. We do it on purpose. Kinda like an initiation. He may be there half the morning. The donut shop is owned by a Chinese family. They speak very little English, but they make great donuts. I sure would like to be a fly on the wall about now."

Jake laughed.

"That's just plain mean," said Vicky. "You fellows should be ashamed of yourselves."

"It's a man thing," said Jake. "It's all in fun."

"Yeah, fun if the joke isn't on you," said Vicky as she turned to leave. "Talk to you later, Jim. Bye now."

As Jake and Vicky were leaving the station, a young man with flaming red, unruly hair was just getting out of one of the undercover cars. He walked around to the passenger side door, reached inside, and took out several boxes marked Ming Pin Donuts. Jake and Vicky stood and watched as the young man carefully carried the stack of boxes into the station. As he passed them on the steps, he smiled and bid them good morning. The smell of fresh donuts filled the air. Vicky's mouth began to water. She turned to Jake.

"I would love a fresh donut about now. Let's see if we can locate a donut shop. There must be one close by."

As the young man was trying to open the door, he overheard what Vicky had said. With his knees bent and his arms full of donut boxes, he turned to them.

"If you want donuts from this particular donut shop, you will have to go clean across town. I must have passed five or six different donut shops on my way there. Ming Pin Donuts must be really good because everyone in the precinct said it was the only place in Birmingham, if you want to get the best donuts."

Jake and Vicky looked at one another and began to snicker. Feeling sorry for the young man, who was obviously Jim's new partner, Andy, Vicky walked back up the steps and opened the door for him.

"Thank you, ma'am," he said politely. "I'd sure hate to drop these and have to go back for more."

As he started to enter, he turned back and said to Vicky, "By the way, the donut shop is on Twenty-Second Avenue."

Vicky thanked him, held the door until he was inside, and joined her husband at the bottom of the stairs. "I don't think I want donuts bad enough to go all the way to

Twenty-Second Avenue. The Krispy Kreme down the road from our house is good enough for me."

Jake agreed.

4

Morning News

Monday morning came without hearing a word from Detective Crawford. Jake and Vicky were getting ready for work. The TV in their bedroom was on the local news channel. Jake had just begun to brush his teeth when Vicky called out to him.

"Jake, come quick. There's a special news report coming on. Maybe it's something new about the murder in Trussville."

Jake peeked out the bathroom door. Across the blue and red screen were plastered the words *Breaking News* in brilliant white letters. Next, the camera went to a small-built, dark-haired woman in a red suit sitting behind a desk. Behind her on the wall was an early morning scene of a nice brick house with a well-manicured yard. Several police cars and an ambulance were parked out front. There was also the familiar face of Stacey Ferguson standing by to give a report.

"Good morning, Birmingham. This is Paula Poole with Channel Six News. Stacey Ferguson is standing by with the report of another brutal murder that has taken place. This time it is in the garden district near Vestavia Hills. Stacey."

"Good morning, Paula. I am here on Wisteria Street where police say another victim has been brutally murdered in much the same way as the murder we reported last week in the Trussville area. The body was discovered by the victim's mother when she came by earlier this morning to bring the victim's two-year-old daughter back from an overnight stay at grandma's house. The name of the victim will not be released until the next of kin can be notified. I spoke briefly to the victim's mother. As you might expect, she was quite upset. I asked her where her son-in-law was at the time of the murder, and she told me he is away on a business trip to Japan. Vestavia Hills is not in Detective Jim Crawford's precinct. However, since the two murders are so closely related, he has been called in to aid in the investigation. When I asked Detective Crawford about the latest murder, he declined to comment. Back to you, Paula."

The camera went back to Paula Poole. "Thank you, Stacey, for that report. We will break with any new information as it comes in. Paula Poole, Channel Six News."

Vicky reached into her closet and pulled out a red maternity top and a pair of navy blue slacks. After laying her outfit on the bed, she called out to Jake, "Can you believe it? Less than a week later and there's already been another murder. I bet this one will make front page, especially being in the Vestavia Hills area. Maybe now, Fred will give me the story."

Jake spit the toothpaste from his mouth, but before rinsing, he spoke in a garbled voice, "You're probably right on both accounts. There may be a serial killer on the loose. Fred would never let an amateur like Brandon handle a story like that."

Vicky sat down on the side of the bed and reached for her pants with the special spandex panel in front, the kind made especially for pregnant woman. As she was bending over to put them on, she realized how difficult just bending over had become. "Of course I'm right. And I can tell you this. I don't care what Fred says, I am going to get this story regardless of my pregnancy. I'm not dead. I'm having a baby."

At about the same time Vicky got her pants pulled up and was pulling her shirt over her head, Jake walked out of the bathroom with nothing on but his underwear and a T-shirt. Vicky smiled and whistled. Jake grinned, held up his arms, and flexed his muscles. Vicky straightened her clothes, walked over to him, and put her arms around his waist.

"Do you still think I'm pretty, Jake?"

Jake wrapped his arms around Vicky. "No," he answered as he looked deeply into Vicky's eyes. "I think you're beautiful. You're even more beautiful than the day we met.

I love you with all my heart, and I can hardly wait until our baby is born so we can hold him or her and I can love our baby as much as I love you."

Vicky laid her head on Jake's chest. "I love you too, Jake."

Jake looked at the clock on the nightstand beside the bed. "Vicky, honey, I'd love to stand here all day and cradle you in my arms, but it's a quarter till nine, and I'm going to be late for work."

Vicky released her hold on him and backed away. "Oh my goodness! I didn't realize it is so late. I need to get to work too. I've got a story to investigate."

Jake pulled on his pants and began buttoning his shirt. Suddenly, he stopped. "Vicky, I know you want to report these murders, and to do that, you have to get as close to them as possible. Just remember, you have to be careful. If anything were to happen to you, I don't know if I could stand it."

Vicky slipped on a pair of navy blue loafers. "Don't worry, honey. I'll be careful. You be careful too. Don't let Mrs. Peacock talk you into leaving me and marrying her."

They both laughed. Vicky gave her hair a quick brushing and applied a dab of lipstick to her lips. Jake grabbed his briefcase, gave Vicky a quick good-bye kiss, and in a flash, they were out the door and on their way.

Jake walked into the building where he worked just seconds before the clock on the wall behind the receptionist's desk read nine o'clock. As he scurried past Betty, she called to him.

"Good morning, Mr. Tillery."

Jake smiled and bid her good morning. Most mornings he would have stopped and chatted for a minute or two, but not this time. Lyndsay Cannon had taken the morning off to see her gynecologist. He was to take care of her appointments until she returned. As he was unlocking his office door, he was relieved to see Mrs. Peacock was not among them. He never knew when she was going to show up, and even though she was one of his favorite clients, her unexpected visits could be bothersome at times. Among those who were on Lyndsay's appointment list was Judas Solomon.

Jake noticed Judas had moved his chair away from the others and was sitting alone. His tan hat was pulled low across his forehead. His arms folded tightly across his chest. Jake also noticed how quiet his other clients were. Normally, they would have been talking to one another, but not that morning. Instead, they all sat quietly awaiting his arrival.

Once the door was unlocked, Jake went inside and laid his briefcase on his desk. Stepping around his desk, he reached for his appointment list. First on the list was Tammy Ewing. Tammy was one of Jake's saddest cases. She had eight children ranging in age from one to thirteen. Her husband had worked for the Birmingham Coal Mining Company until his untimely death six months ago. Tammy had no work skills, and with nine mouths to feed, she had applied for assistance from the state. Jake felt if anyone deserved assistance, it was Tammy. As he was about to ask her to come in, the door opened. However, it was not Tammy Ewing. It was Judas Solomon.

"Mr. Solomon," Jake announced curtly. "How are you this morning?"

Without answering, Judas walked across the room and sat down in the chair opposite Jake's desk. Jake did not like his demeanor, or his presumption that he could just walk in any time he pleased. However, he tried being hospitable.

"I'm glad to see you're showing up for your appointments, Mr. Solomon. However, you are two hours early, and I have several people to see before you."

Judas did not move nor did he respond.

"Did you hear me, Mr. Solomon? I said, I have several people in front of you. If you would be so kind as to have a seat in the hallway, I will be with you shortly."

Still, Judas did not make any effort to leave. Instead, he pushed his hat back from his forehead and glared at Jake with a blank-eyed stare. Jake felt chills run down his spine. Never before had he felt afraid of one of his clients. After all, he was there to help them, and most of them appreciated the help. Still, he could not, nor would not, let

Judas intimidate him. Just as he was about to insist Judas should leave and wait his turn, Judas spoke.

"Have ya got me another place to live yet? That stinkin' apartment y'all got me ain't nothin' but a sorry excuse for a jail cell. I need a place whar I can have some privacy. The bed is hard. Ain't fit fer a dog much less a man."

Jake was shocked at the nerve of Judas.

"I wasn't aware that you were displeased with your accommodations, Mr. Solomon. What—"

Judas interrupted, "And them checks I git ain't near 'nuff to live off of. That little fifty dollars a week mess don't git it."

Normally, Jake was a very patient man, but Judas was wearing his patience thin.

"What do all y'all do round here all day? Twiddle your thumbs?" sassed Judas.

Suddenly, Jake's fear and his tolerance flew right out the window.

"Listen here, Mr. Solomon," he roared. "You're not the only client we have. Do you see that stack of files? All those files are people who need our help. And those are only Mrs. Cannon's clients. They are people who, unlike yourself, have never been in prison. They are simply people down on their luck. Our job is to see to it they have a helping hand until they can get back on their feet. Our job is not to make sure a known killer is pampered and petted with the best of everything. Now…I am willing and ready to help you anyway I can, but neither I nor Mrs. Cannon are going to put your needs ahead of everyone else. You have a place to live and you have money to spend. You get food stamps and free medical. All you have to do is show up for your appointments. You will live where we say you will live. And you will be respectful to me, to Mrs. Cannon, and to the people ahead of you. Otherwise, you can go back to prison, where frankly, I think you should still be. Is that understood, Mr. Solomon?"

Jake could tell Judas did not appreciate his lecture nor did he care about anyone but himself. Judas responded by curling his lip in a snarl and growled like the dog he was. Jake moved around his desk and took a stance beside the chair where Judas continued to sit. Jake reached down and took hold of his upper arm. As he was trying to lift Judas out of the chair, Judas snatched his arm from Jake's hold and stood defiantly on his own. Once again, the hair on the back of Jake's neck stood on ends. He could feel the fear in him rising, but he knew at that point, he could not back down from Judas's terrifying blank stare.

For what seemed like several minutes, they stared at one another, eyeball to eyeball. Neither man wanted to be the first to back down. Jake did not want to back down because he knew he had to show Judas he could not disrespect him. Judas wouldn't back down simply because he wanted to be in control. As they stood face-to-face only inches apart, the door suddenly opened, and Hoss, the security guard, was standing there.

His real name was Joe Johnson, but everyone called him Hoss. He was an African-American, very dark skinned with deep-set, dark brown eyes and black close-cropped hair. He stood six-feet-four-inches tall with massive muscles that bulged out from beneath his short-sleeved uniform shirt. He spoke in a deep intimidating voice.

"Is this feller givin' ya' trouble, Mr. Tillery?" he asked.

Still not breaking his stare, Jake answered, "No, Hoss. Mr. Solomon was just leaving. Isn't that right, Mr. Solomon?"

Judas sneered at Jake one final time and turned to leave. Hoss stepped aside but watched closely as Judas headed for the door. Just before leaving, Judas turned to Jake. "Better watch yourself, Jake. Remember, I'm a killer ya know."

Hoss grabbed Judas by the arm and bent it upward behind his back. "Ya better watch yourself, little man," he scolded. "Best ya get on out of here 'fore I have to put ya in your place."

When Hoss and Judas were out of sight, Jake sat down at his desk to compose himself. His heart was pounding in his chest. His hands were sweaty. Never before had he felt afraid of one of his clients. His thoughts were interrupted when Mrs. Porter entered the room.

"Is everything all right in here, Jake?" she asked, standing just inside the doorway.

"Everything has been taken care of. Thank you, Mrs. Porter," Jake said, his voice trembling slightly.

"Why are all these people outside your office?"

Jake reached for the appointment book, scanned the page, and asked Mrs. Porter to have Mrs. Raymond come in.

"Where is Mrs. Cannon?" Mrs. Porter asked sharply.

"She had a doctor's appointment this morning. She asked me to see her clients for her. She will be in after lunch."

"What was that commotion I heard going on down here a few minutes ago?"

Jake looked directly at Mrs. Porter before answering, "That was Judas Solomon. He's the man I told you was going to give Lyndsay trouble. Thank goodness I was here today to deal with him instead of her. I don't know what she would have done."

"Are you saying Mrs. Cannon can't do her job, Jake?"

"I'm saying nothing of the kind, Mrs. Porter. I'm saying Judas Solomon is not your everyday case. He is a convicted felon. The last thing Lyndsay needs to be dealing with in her condition is a man like Judas."

"Fine then," answered Mrs. Porter. "If you think it's best you handle Mr. Solomon, then so be it. Just get this hallway cleared out as quickly as possible. The review board is coming by today. The last thing we need is a hallway full of clients waiting to be seen."

Jake nodded his head in agreement. "I'll do my best. If you would, ask Mrs. Raymond to come in, please."

Two months passed by. Regrettably, there had been two more murders of young women in the Birmingham area. Each of them had been murdered in the same manner as the first two. The third victim was a homeless woman in her midthirties, who was living out of her car on the north side of town. Very little was known about her except that her car had an expired Florida tag on the rear bumper. However, it was the fourth murder victim that caused a big stir.

Her name was Sarah Anne Young. She's the daughter of city councilman Blake Seamon. Her well-to-do husband, Dallis Young, was out of town on a business trip. The family maid discovered her body lying facedown in the kitchen of their upscale condominium. The mayor immediately called for a task force to be assembled, which would be headed by Detective Jim Crawford. The mayor made the announcement on the midday news.

"It's about time!" Vicky exclaimed. "There should have already been a task force working on these cases."

Jake was standing at the kitchen counter making both of them a ham and cheese sandwich for lunch.

"I guess they needed to come to the realization that they are dealing with a serial killer."

"No. They needed someone of so-called importance, like the councilman's daughter, to get murdered before they reacted."

Jake sat the sandwich on the table in front of Vicky. "You're probably right, Vick."

"I know I'm right. As long as the women being killed were poor, no one really cared. One less homeless person, one less drug addict."

"What about the woman in Vestavia Hills? She wasn't poor."

"No, but she wasn't rich either or tied to some politician's apron strings."

"Aren't we being a might sarcastic this morning?" Jake replied jokingly.

Vicky stood up, walked over to the refrigerator, opened the door, and took out a carton of 2 percent milk. While getting the milk, she spied a jar of dill pickles and immediately decided she had to have one with her sandwich. Since both her hands were full, she closed the refrigerator door with her barefoot and then turned and sat the jar of pickles and the milk on the counter.

"It just makes me mad when city officials wait so long to do something that should have been done from the beginning. I mean, Jim is a good detective, but he and Andy can't do a big case like this one all by themselves."

Jake took a bite from his sandwich. "Well, at least now they'll have help," he commented in a rather garbled voice.

Vicky sat down at the table next to him. "Jake, don't talk with your mouth full. It's not polite," Vicky scolded.

Jake smiled. "Yes, Mother."

Vicky abruptly stopped pouring milk into her glass and looked at Jake. "Oh my goodness. I'm already starting to sound just like my mother, and I'm not even a mother yet."

Jake laughed. "Yep. Our poor kid is in for it. I can tell already."

Vicky teasingly slapped Jake on the back of his hand.

After lunch, Jake decided he would spend the afternoon working in the yard. Just as he was about to go outside, the phone rang. He reluctantly answered it.

"Hello. Tillery residence."

"Good mornin'. This is Jerry Cook from New Prospect Church. Is this Jake Tillery?"

"It is indeed, Mr. Cook. How are you?"

"I'm fair to middlin'," he answered. "Sorry it's taken me so long to get back to you about the cemetery lot beside Stella Hubert."

"That's fine, Mr. Cook. What has the church decided?"

"Well, at first they were against it. But I done some talkin' and we all done some prayin' and it was finally decided that we would allow Rose to be moved next to Stella. It just seemed like the Christian thing to do."

"That is great news, Mr. Cook. I will contact the cemetery in Tuscaloosa to see about making arrangements for transporting her remains."

"That's fine. But now you do understand she will have to be in a vault. Most of them pauper cemeteries don't require being in a vault, but we do. We did that several years back when some of the graves started caving in, exposing the caskets and even some skeletons."

"I understand completely, Mr. Cook. You can rest assured I will make sure her casket is put into a vault and a headstone placed at the head of her grave."

"Very good. Just let me know when, and I'll get Bubba to dig a hole to put her in."

"Thank you very much, Mr. Cook. I will certainly be in touch. Have a nice day."

"Yeah. You too. Good-bye now."

When Jake hung up, he told Vicky about the decision and then immediately called Benton Mental Institution to make arrangements for Rose to be moved to New Prospect Cemetery. He was told the cost of exhuming her and transporting her by way of a hearse would cost approximately six hundred dollars. Jake gave them his credit card information and was told they would deliver the body to New Prospect Cemetery Monday morning around ten.

He called Mr. Cook back and gave him the information he'd been given. Mr. Cook confirmed that the lot would be ready, and that Jake would need to pay Bubba one hundred dollars on completion of the job. Jake agreed he would have the money and would be there by nine Monday morning to make sure a vault was delivered, meet the hearse, pay Bubba, and, lastly, to lay Rose to rest beside her old friend.

When he hung up the phone with Mr. Cook, he immediately called Bernice Stapler to give her the good news. She was pleased and delighted to know about the moving of Rose to her new resting place. She thanked Jake again and again. She was truly relieved to know she was able to keep her promise to Stella and that she would rest beside Rose for all eternity.

5

Disappearing One at a Time

It seemed to Jake that everywhere he looked, there were pregnant women. Vicky's belly was so big she looked as though she was about to pop open at any second. Lyndsay was almost as big around as she was tall. However, she waddled into work on time every morning. Besides Vicky and Lyndsay, there were two other office workers who were pregnant and so was the security guard's wife. Jake teased them saying it had to be in the drinking water. Betty, the file clerk, was not married and refused to drink anything but fruit juice and diet sodas.

Vicky's car had been giving her trouble for several days, so Jake decided to drop her off at the newspaper office and then take her car in for repairs at the garage two doors down from his building. He was fifteen minutes late getting to work and was completely surprised to see the hallway full of people in front of Lyndsay's office. He certainly didn't remember her asking him to take her clients. *Perhaps she's had her baby*, he thought.

As he passed by the reception desk, he called out to Betty, "Where's Lyndsay?"

Betty was on the phone but covered the receiver to answer him.

"I don't know. I've tried to call her at her home, but no one answers. I'm trying to find out. I've got the hospital operator checking to see if she's in the maternity ward. She's got a full load today. It's not like her not to call."

Betty held up her hand to let Jake know the operator was back on the line. "Are you sure?" she asked. "Well, thank you for checking. Yes, good-bye."

"Not at the hospital?" Jake asked.

"No. Should I call her husband?"

"If she doesn't come in by lunchtime, you can call him. I suspect she's either on her way or maybe she had a doctor's appointment this morning and just forgot to tell us. I'll handle her cases until she gets here or until we find out what the deal is."

Jake got busy helping the people waiting to see Lyndsay. Time passed by quickly as one after the other came and went. When all the clients on the morning schedule had been seen, Jake walked down the hall to the front desk. Betty looked distressed.

"Have you heard anything from Lyndsay yet?" he asked.

"I just got off the phone with her husband. He said she was getting dressed to go to work when he left for work this morning. He's really worried too. What should I do, Mr. Tillery?"

Jake thought for a moment. "Give me Lyndsay's home address. I've got to pick up our car from the garage. I'll drop by her house and see what I can find out. She may have had car trouble too."

"I hope that's all it is," said Betty.

Jake was walking out the door just as Vicky drove up in front of the building and blew her horn. Obviously, she had already picked up the car. Jake hurriedly opened the door and got inside.

"What are you doing here?"

"They called from the garage and said the car was ready, so I had Brandon drop me off. Where are you headed?"

"Lyndsay didn't show up for work this morning."

"Maybe she's having her baby."

"Betty called the hospital, her doctor's office, and even her husband's work. Terry said she was getting ready to go to work when he left. I thought I would drop by and see if I could find out anything."

"Good deal. I don't have anything going right now. I'll take you."

Jake and Vicky drove the two-mile trip to Lyndsay's house. It was a rather small white house with dark green shutters. It looked as though it had recently been painted. The yard was well groomed and edged neatly along the walkway.

"Cute house," Vicky remarked as she parked the car out front alongside the curb.

"Yeah," Jake agreed. "I like this neighborhood. It's a quiet older neighborhood. I understand more young people are moving in as the older people die off."

There was a slightly dilapidated garage at the end of the drive, but it was obvious it was not being used to shelter the cars as it was full of lawnmowers, garden hoes, rakes, gas cans, and the like. Lyndsay's car was nowhere to be seen.

"It doesn't appear she's at home. At least her car isn't here," Vicky noted.

"Terry might have taken it. Let's check to see if she's here, being we're here anyway."

As they approached the front steps, Vicky noticed the front door was slightly ajar.

"That's odd," she remarked.

Jake was looking at the gardenia bush growing near the right corner of the house. It looked as though some of the branches had been broken recently.

"What's odd?" he asked, his attention still on the bush.

"The front door is open."

Jake's attention immediately went from the broken branches on the bush to the open door. As they stepped onto the porch, Jake took the lead. "Let me go in first. Better yet, you stay out here while I investigate."

"Not on your life, Jake Tillery. I'm sticking to you like white on rice. I'm a reporter. Remember?"

Jake pushed open the door. It opened into a narrow hallway. To his left was the living room. To his right the dining room. Nothing seemed to be amiss. Before going any farther, he called out, "Lyndsay! Are you home? It's Jake and Vicky. Lyndsay!"

The house was silent. They could see there were lights on in one of the rooms down the hall. Side by side they slowly made their way down the hall. The first room they came to was a bathroom. The door was open, but everything looked perfectly normal. Next, they came to a bedroom. Vicky pushed the door open to reveal a baby's room. It had been freshly painted blue with a teddy bear border along the top of the room. An oak baby bed sat near the window. The sheets and comforter had teddy bears that matched the border. A teddy bear mobile hung over the head of the bed. A rather large brown teddy bear sat in a rocking chair beside the window.

"I think they like teddy bears," Vicky whispered.

Next to the baby's room was the room where the light was on. The door was open. They peeked inside. Unlike the rest of the house, which was neat and organized, this room was in total chaos. Overturned tables, a broken lamp lying on the floor near the bed, a curtain partly torn from the window. The blue princess-style telephone had been ripped from the connection and was lying across the disheveled bed. Lyndsay was nowhere to be seen.

"Oh my gosh!" Vicky exclaimed. "Jake! Something terrible has happened here! We need to call the police immediately."

"You're right, Vick," Jake agreed. "See if you can find a working phone. I'll check the other rooms."

Vicky found another phone hanging on the wall in the kitchen. She picked it up and dialed 911. When the emergency operator answered, Vicky asked to be connected to the police. While she was explaining to the police operator what they had found, Jake searched the house for any clues as to the whereabouts of Lyndsay. The other bedroom and the laundry room were undisturbed. However, in the hallway between the bedrooms was a linen closet. The door was open, and it appeared that something had been haphazardly removed from it. Less than five minutes later, a squad car and an unmarked car arrived in front of the house. The unmarked car was that of Detective Jim Crawford and his partner, Andy. Jake and Vicky were waiting outside on the porch when they arrived. Jim took the steps, two at a time. Andy followed closely behind.

"What's going on?" he asked. "Who lives here?"

Jake spoke first.

"Terry and Lyndsay Cannon. Lyndsay is one of the social workers where I work. She took my job when I got promoted. When she didn't show up for work this morning, Betty, our receptionist, called her but got no answer. She also called to Terry's workplace. He said she was getting ready for work when he left this morning. Betty even called the hospital. Vicky and I decided to check on her."

"Why would she call the hospital?" Andy asked.

"She's eight months pregnant," Vicky answered. "We thought she might have gone into labor and didn't have time to call anyone."

Jim got a very disturbed look on his face. "Pregnant you say? Huh. Well, let's take a look inside." He opened the door. "You two didn't touch anything, did you?"

"No. Nothing," said Jake.

Vicky quickly corrected him. "I did touch the phone in the kitchen. I used it to call 911."

Jim turned to the policemen who were still standing at the edge of the steps. "Get in touch with the crime lab. Have them come over immediately to check for fingerprints."

As Jake, Vicky, Andy, and Jim were making their way down the hall, Vicky called to Jim. "Jim, why did you say 'huh' when I told you Lyndsay was pregnant? You got a strange look on your face too."

Jim stopped dead still and looked at Vicky. "This has to be off the record, Vicky. We don't need to alarm every pregnant woman in Jefferson County. Understood?"

"Understood," she replied.

"All four women who have been killed were also pregnant."

Vicky turned pale. "You're joking. Right?"

"It's no joke, Vicky," Jim replied. "We've tried to keep that bit of information out of the hands of the press. Like I said, we don't want to panic anyone."

Jake was surprised too. He thought back on his own mother being murdered when she was pregnant. "What about the babies, Jim?"

"The babies were dead too. We found them lying beside the women's bodies."

"How far along were the pregnancies?" Jake asked.

"Hard to say," Andy said. "Forensics put them somewhere in the five- to seven-month range."

Jim started moving down the hall. When they got to Lyndsay's bedroom, Jim and Andy went into the room to inspect it. Shortly afterward, Bill Bailey from the fingerprint lab arrived and began dusting for prints. Vicky and Jake decided it was time to leave. Just as they were getting to the car, Terry pulled up, turned off the ignition, jumped out of his truck, and ran over to them.

"What are the police doing here?" he asked panicked. "Did you find Lyndsay?"

Jake laid his arm across Terry's shoulder. "No, Terry, we haven't found her yet. However, it does appear someone might have taken her."

Terry was in anguish. "Taken her?" he yelled. "Who would want to take her? What do you mean taken her?"

As Jake was trying to calm Terry down, Vicky noticed someone, who looked like a woman, peeking out the window from the house directly across the street. She decided to go and talk to her. Perhaps she might have seen or heard something or someone. As soon as she stepped onto the porch, the front door opened and there stood a short, elderly, white-haired lady in a pink cotton house dress, pink fuzzy bedroom slippers, and wearing very thick horn-rimmed glasses.

Vicky smiled.

"Good day," Vicky said, as the woman pushed open the screen door. "I'm Vicky Tillery with the Birmingham News. May I take a moment of your time to ask a few questions?"

The lady smiled back. "Yes, of course, dear. Come in, won't you?"

Vicky stepped inside. Six cats of every age and color came out of nowhere and began rubbing up against her legs, purring.

"Please, don't mind my babies," the lady said. "They're very friendly, and we don't get much company. They're just welcoming you."

The lady in pink motioned for Vicky to follow her. Stepping carefully around the cats, Vicky followed her into the sitting area. The room was very clean, but it smelled musty, like old blankets after they've been stored in the attic. The furniture was definitely antique but had been well cared for. The coffee and end tables were mahogany. Not the reproduction kind, but pure mahogany wood, rich with color like that of polished chestnut hull. The sofa was

Victorian, covered in lush gold velvet. Above the mantle hung a large oil painting of a handsome, young, dark-haired man and a petite young blonde woman. They appeared to be in their early to midthirties. The woman noticed Vicky looking at it.

"That was me and my husband, Benjamin, back in our younger days. He was a handsome devil. Wasn't he?"

Vicky smiled. "Yes. Very handsome indeed. You have a lovely home."

The lady sat down in a high-back chair that matched the sofa and motioned Vicky to have a seat on the sofa. As Vicky was sitting down, the lady spoke again.

"Where are my manners? Would you care for some tea?"

"Oh no, that's very kind of you, but I wouldn't care for tea. I would like to ask you a few questions though."

"Certainly, dear."

"Do you mind telling me your name?"

"I'm Mrs. Benjamin Dalton Brock," she said proudly. "My given name is Melissa. However, you may call me Missy. It's a nickname you know."

Although calling an elderly person by a nickname felt rather odd for Vicky's southern upbringing, she felt obliged to do so. "Okay, Missy. Were you at home this morning?"

"Oh yes. Just me and my precious cats."

"Did you happen to notice anything unusual going on across the street?"

Missy straightened her dress neatly across her lap. "As a matter of fact, I did. It was shortly after I heard Terry leave for work. He leaves around six in the morning. I heard his old rickety truck pull out of the driveway. Sometimes it backfires and scares my poor cats nearly to death. A short time later, I believe it was around six-thirty...I know because I had just finished watching the six o'clock news, I turned off the TV and went to the door to let Scooter out. He's my oldest cat. He likes to wander the neighborhood first thing in the morning. The neighbors have spoiled him. They give him a treat every time he drops by, so he's always anxious to go on his morning walkabout. As I was letting him out, I looked toward Lyndsay's house to see if she had also left for work. That was when I noticed someone carrying something very large across her yard. I don't see too well, so I couldn't say who it was I saw, but I knew it wasn't Lyndsay. She would never be carrying something so big. She's pregnant you know. Terry hardly lets her pick up the mail or the newspaper for fear it's too heavy. It's very sweet, but Lyndsay says he's driving her crazy being so overprotective." She paused. "It will be so nice to have a baby living across the street. I told Lyndsay I would be glad to babysit for her anytime she needs me. I love little babies. They smell so sweet, like Johnson's baby powder."

Vicky didn't know whether she should tell Missy about Lyndsay's disappearance or not. Missy had said she watches the news and most assuredly it would be on the evening news. Consequently, she decided it was best to let her know before she heard about it while watching TV.

"Missy, Lyndsay is missing. She didn't show up for work this morning. She works with my husband, Jake. When she didn't come in to work, we came to check on her."

Missy looked very disturbed. "Oh my! I do hope she's all right. She loves her job. She's such a sweet girl. She and Terry are always doing things for me. Terry cuts my grass every week and doesn't charge me anything. I try to pay him, but he won't take a penny. He loves my five flavor pound cake, so I repay him by baking him a cake. Oh dear. This is not good. Do you think someone kidnapped her?"

"We're not sure yet, but it appears that way. Did you see the person leave in some kind of vehicle?"

"No, I didn't. After I let Scooter out, I closed the door and went to the kitchen to fix my breakfast. I always have a bowl of oatmeal with blueberries on top. Benjamin used to tease me about turning into a bowl of oatmeal and blueberries. They say blueberries are good for you, you know."

"So you didn't see anyone leave in Lyndsay's car?"

"No. By the time I had my breakfast, Scooter was at the door wanting to come back in. I looked across the street and Lyndsay's car was gone. I assumed she had left for work. If only I had paid more attention. I certainly hope nothing bad has happened to her."

"Me too, Missy." Vicky rose to her feet. "I need to go now. If you think of anything else, please call me. Okay?"

Missy stood up also. One of the cats walked up alongside her and began rubbing against her leg. She looked down. "Prissy wants to be fed. I haven't fed them their lunch yet."

Vicky smiled and handed Missy her business card. "My work number and home phone number are on the card."

Missy took the card and walked with Vicky to the door. "I do hope you find her soon. Please tell Terry he is welcome to come over if he needs to talk or if I can help in any way."

"I will, Missy, and thanks again for talking to me."

That evening, all the TV stations from around the state were headlining the news about the missing Birmingham woman. Although Detective Crawford had tried to keep the fact that Lyndsay, as well as the other four women, were pregnant out of the news, it was obvious someone had leaked the information. Vicky knew it was neither she nor Jake, but she had her suspicions who did. Her hunch was confirmed when she saw Melissa Brock on the Channel Six News that evening. She was holding Scooter in her arms and telling Stacey Ferguson about seeing someone carrying something big across the yard that morning.

Vicky and Jake were preparing dinner. They were making Chinese stir-fry. She was cutting a variety of vegetables into thin slices on her cutting board while Jake was preparing to put the rice on to cook.

"Jake, this is terrible," she said. "I feel so bad for Terry. I know he must be out of his mind with worry."

Jake set the pot on the stove and turned on the heat beneath it. "I know. Everyone at work can't stop talking about it. I wish there was more we could do."

"If only we had some idea of who might have taken her and why."

"Don't you find it odd that Lyndsay was taken from her home and the other four women were not? Instead, they were all found where the killer murdered them. It doesn't make sense. Why would he take Lyndsay and not the others?"

"That's a very good question, Jake. I hadn't even thought about it that way."

"Maybe he's hiding her somewhere, and the police will find her alive."

"That would be wonderful!" replied Vicky.

"All we can do right now is continue to pray for both Lyndsay and Terry."

When Monday morning arrived, there was still no word on the whereabouts of Lyndsay Cannon. Jake wanted desperately to spend the day looking for her, but he knew he would have to take care of Jefferson County's business first. When he arrived, Betty handed him Lyndsay's schedule for the day. He thanked her and started down the hall. The atmosphere in the building was bleak. No one was wishing the other a good morning or standing by the coffee machine cracking jokes, as was customary first thing in the morning. When Jake reached his office, he laid his briefcase down on his desk and surveyed the schedule. At the top of the list was Judas Solomon. *Not Judas Solomon*, he thought. *He is the last person I want to have to deal with this morning.*

After making a couple of necessary calls, Jake reluctantly went to the door to get Judas. To his surprise, Judas was not present. He stepped into the hallway to see if he was sitting in front of Lyndsay's office. He was not. *Okay*, he thought. *Wonder where our dear Mr. Solomon is this morning.* The next person on his list was sitting quietly, patiently awaiting her turn. He turned to her and put out his hand. "I'm Jake Tillery, Mrs. Summersgill. I'll be talking to you today. Please come in."

Mrs. Summersgill preceded Jake into his office and took the seat across from his desk. "I heard about Mrs. Cannon's disappearance on TV," she said shyly. "I hope they find her soon. She's a very nice person. I hope whoever has her hasn't killed her."

"We feel the same way, Mrs. Summersgill. Have you noticed anyone giving her a hard time recently?"

"Well"—she paused and looked over her shoulder as though she was making sure no one was listening—"that odd man that always wears a hat pulled low across his face."

"You mean, Judas Solomon?"

"Yes. I think I've heard Mrs. Cannon call him that. He's always making vulgar remarks while we're waiting to see Mrs. Cannon. I was glad to see he wasn't here this morning."

"Have you heard him making vulgar remarks to, Mrs. Cannon?"

"No. Just to those of us waiting in the hallway."

"What kind of remarks does he say to you and the others?"

"Please, Mr. Tillery, I'd rather not repeat them."

Jake could see Mrs. Summersgill was getting anxious about his questioning. "That's fine. I get the idea. No more questions about Mr. Solomon, okay?"

Mrs. Summersgill smiled. "Thank you."

"Now, how are things going with you and your children?"

The day went by very quickly. Jake was winding things down when his phone rang. "Hello. This is Jake Tillery."

"Mr. Tillery, this is Tom Denny. I understand you are the man I need to speak to about one of my parolees, Judas Solomon."

"Yes. I am, Mr. Denny. What can I do for you?"

"Well, our Mr. Solomon has not showed up for his last two check-ins. I was wondering if you'd seen him?"

Jake explained to Mr. Denny that Lyndsay had been assigned to Mr. Solomon's case, but that he had taken over for her clients in her absence. He also advised him that Mr. Solomon had not shown up for his appointment that morning.

"I see," replied Mr. Denny. "Is Mrs. Cannon the same person the police are looking for?"

"Yes."

"And she's pregnant?"

"Yes."

There was a moment of silence on the other end of the line.

"Mr. Tillery, are you aware of what Judas Solomon was in prison for?"

"I believe he killed a young woman."

"Yes, Mr. Tillery. A young pregnant woman by the name of Ginny Macon. And she was not just killed. She was brutally murdered, beaten to death, and shot in the head with a shotgun. The baby she had carried for nine months was cut from her abdomen. A week later, they caught Judas and arrested him for her murder, but they never found the poor woman's baby. They suspected him of selling the baby on the black market, but they were never able to prove it. What made matters even worse, she had been raped nine months earlier, and the baby she was carrying was a result of that rape."

"Did they catch her rapist?"

"That's the weird part. After Solomon was convicted of murder and was in prison, he told his cellmate that he had raped Miss Macon and the baby she was carrying was his. When the other prisoner asked him what he did with the baby, he said he wasn't saying, and no one would ever find it."

Jake was in shock. "Oh my Lord! How awful! And to think the parole board let a madman like him out on parole."

"It's beyond me," Mr. Denny agreed. "They should have electrocuted him. Better yet, taken him out back of the jail and beat him to death."

"I should have read his file more closely. I would never have allowed Lyndsay to have taken his case. I wanted to keep the case, but my supervisor insisted he be turned over to Lyndsay."

"The police will be lucky to find her alive."

"God, I hope she hasn't fallen into his hands."

"We can only hope," replied Mr. Denny. "I'll let you know if I hear from him, and I trust you will do the same."

"Absolutely. Thank you for calling."

When Jake hung up the phone, he was shaking. This was an absolute travesty of justice. He was angry. He was angry with the prison system for turning a rapist and killer loose. He was angry with Mrs. Porter for insisting Lyndsay take Judas's case, and he was angry with himself for letting her take it. If it was Judas Solomon who took Lyndsay, and if Judas had killed her, he knew he would never be able to forgive himself. He had to find her. He had to find Lyndsay Cannon.

Jake decided it was time to devote every waking minute to finding Lyndsay. He had several days of vacation time left, so he went to Mrs. Porter to ask for some time off. At first she refused, saying they were already shorthanded and that she needed him there to take care of Lyndsay's cases. However, when the rest of the staff came to his rescue, assuring her they would divide Lyndsay's clients among them, she had no choice but to let him take off or end up with an entire office full of disgruntled employees. Jake thanked all of them and immediately went to work, finding out all he could about Judas Solomon.

The first place he went was to the newspaper office where Vicky worked. She was out on assignment, but when Fred found out what he was doing, he gave Jake full range of whatever information he could dig up from old newspaper clippings and articles. Many of them had been put on computer disks, but the ones older than ten years were still on film. Since Judas had been incarcerated for the past twenty years, he would need to go back to around the time he was sentenced.

As he was scanning the pages, he came across an article about a young woman who was raped. The woman was from Clanton, Alabama. Her name was not given because she was a few months short of eighteen years old and considered a minor. The article went on to say that Sheriff John Thornton believed the rape was committed by someone not from the immediate area. Jake searched for other articles about the rape but was unable to find anything further until he came across an article about a young pregnant woman who had been murdered and the baby she was carrying was missing. The name given was Ginny Macon. Jake recognized the name as being the person who Judas Solomon had killed.

An article printed one week to the day later made headline news: "Man Arrested in the Brutal Murder of a Clanton Woman." The article read:

> Judas Solomon has been arrested for the brutal murder of Ginny Macon, a resident of Clanton, Alabama. Solomon was taken into custody at his rental home in Marbury, after police received an anonymous tip from one of the local residents. When Sheriff John Thornton and his deputies, Coy Rucker and Ralph Meed, went to his house, Solomon was found to be in possession of a sawed-off shotgun and a bloody hatchet. Testing showed the blood to be that of the victim, Ginny Macon. Solomon is being held in the Chilton County jail without bond.

Jake had no sooner finished reading the article when someone touched him on his shoulder and he nearly jumped out of his skin. He quickly turned around to see who it was. Vicky was laughing so hard that tears were rolling down her face.

"Vicky Tillery!" he scolded. "You're gonna give me a heart attack one of these days. You shouldn't sneak up on me like that. You scared me half to death."

Vicky continued laughing so hard she could barely speak. "I'm sorry, Jake, but I just can't help it. You should have seen how far you came up out of that chair. And the look on your face was priceless."

"Well, you're gonna be husbandless if you keep scaring me like that."

Vicky straightened up and tried to compose herself. "I'm truly sorry, honey. I promise I won't do it again."

Jake started to smile. "You lie. You know you'll do it again the first chance you get."

"I know I shouldn't, but it's fun."

"That's all right," Jake warned. "Your turn is coming. Payback is tough."

Vicky decided it was time to change the subject. "What are you looking for in these old newspapers?"

Jake told her about Mr. Denny calling him and about the murder of Ginny Macon. He also told her he had taken time off from work to try and help find Lyndsay.

"I'm with you there, Jake. Where should we start?"

Jake leaned back in his chair. "I think we should go to Judas's apartment first. I have his file in the car. We can get the address and get started on the search for Lyndsay."

"Great! Let me tell Fred where we're going. Since I got pregnant, he gets his panties in a wad if I don't tell him where I'm going at all times."

"Good for Fred. I'm glad he's looking out for you."

Vicky leaned down, kissed Jake on the cheek, and whispered in his ear, "He's almost as bad as you are."

6

Alone

Jake and Vicky arrived at Judas's apartment building around six in the evening. It was beginning to get dusk dark. Jake wanted to find out as much as possible as to the whereabouts of Judas Solomon in as little time as possible. No way did he want to be in the middle of the projects after dark. The crime rate there was off the charts. He was sure it was a place where Judas felt right at home.

The building was three floors high and made of red brick. The trim had been painted white, but it was peeling in places and bare rotting wood was exposed. One of the gutters on the side of the building had come loose and was dangling in midair. Several window screens looked as though they had been cut open with a knife. Some windows had no screen at all. Several men sat on the steps smoking cigarettes and talking.

"Well, this is it," said Jake as he came to a stop in front of the building.

"Kind of rundown, isn't it?"

"Yeah, but it's better than prison I suppose. Most of the men staying here are on parole or have been on parole. Why don't you wait in the car with the doors locked?"

"Not on your life, Jake. You're not leaving me in this car alone. No way."

"Fine, but stay close and try not to stare."

Vicky reached into her purse and took out a small aerosol can. Jake looked puzzled. She held it up to him to reveal a can of pepper spray. Vicky put the can in the pocket of her slacks.

"Hopefully, we won't need this," she said. "But it can't hurt to have it handy."

Jake got out first and went around to the passenger side to open the door for Vicky. The men on the steps fell quiet and watched intently as they made their way up the broken sidewalk. When Jake and Vicky reached the steps, Jake stopped.

"Hello," he said to the man closest to him. "I'm looking for Judas Solomon. Would any of you fellows know where he might be?"

The men looked around at one another. Finally, the older, dark-skinned man spit a streak of amber onto the ground next to the steps before replying, "Why ya' lookin' fer him? You be cops?"

Jake smiled nervously. "No. No. I'm his social worker, Jake Tillery. He didn't show up for his appointment today, so I came by to check on him."

A young man with deep brown eyes and an oversized afro hairstyle spoke next. "He ain't been here three, fo' days now."

"Do any of you know where he might have gone?" asked Vicky.

"Don't know. Don't care," said the older man.

The other men laughed.

Jake could see he was getting nowhere with the men, so he asked them to step aside so he and Vicky could enter. Reluctantly, they slowly slid to one side, allowing them entrance to the building. Once inside, they climbed the well-worn stairs to the second floor. The inside of the building was in worse shape than the outside. Repulsive graffiti covered the walls. The stairs were sticky in places where who-knows-what had been spilled. Vicky carefully stepped around wads of chewing tobacco left here and there on the landing between the first and second floor.

"According to my records, he should be in apartment 212," said Jake.

Vicky followed Jake down the long hallway until they reached apartment 212.

One of the twos had become unattached at the top and was hanging upside down. Jake knocked on the door, but no one answered. He knocked again, only louder. The door to the apartment across the hall opened up, and a young blonde-haired girl, who looked to be around the age of ten, peeked out.

"He's not home," she said shyly.

Vicky turned to her and smiled. "Hi, sweetheart. Do you know where he is?" she asked.

"No," she answered. "And I'm glad he's gone. I don't like him. He says mean things to me and my little sister."

Jake turned to the little girl. "Is your mommy home?"

"No. She went to get some food. We haven't eaten in two whole days."

"Are you alone?" asked Vicky.

"No. My little sister is here with me. She's asleep."

Jake and Vicky looked at one another and then back to the little girl.

"What is your name, honey?" Vicky asked.

"Julie, and my sister's name is Michelle."

"How long has your mommy been gone?" Jake asked.

"I guess she left last night. She wasn't here when we woke up this morning."

"Where's your daddy?" asked Vicky.

"He's asleep too."

Jake handed her one of his business cards. "Will you give this to him and tell him to call me if any of you see Mr. Solomon."

Julie took the card, nodded yes, waved good-bye, and quietly closed the door.

As Jake and Vicky were walking down the stairs to leave the building, Vicky touched Jake's arm. "How do you deal with situations like that every day, Jake? That poor little girl."

"There are hundreds, if not thousands of cases exactly like hers and worse. I'm surprised her dad was home. And in reality, he may not have been home at all. Sometimes these latchkey kids are told to lie about being left alone so welfare won't come and take them away for being left unattended. I've got the address, so I will check to see if in fact there is a father figure present in the apartment. If not, I'll put in a call to child welfare."

When they reached the front of the building, the same men were still sitting on the steps. Jake took a business card from his jacket pocket and handed it to the older man. "If Mr. Solomon happens to come around, how about giving me a call?"

"Phone calls cost money," the young black man intervened.

Jake looked at Vicky, reluctantly took out his wallet, and handed him a five-dollar bill.

"Maybe this will help pay for the call," said Jake.

The young man put the money in his shirt pocket. "Maybe," he said with a slight smirk on his face.

Jake and Vicky bid them good day and headed back to the car. When they were safely inside and the doors locked, they each breathed a little easier. Jake worked with underprivileged people every day, but it was usually on his terms and in his space and not theirs. Since his promotion, he'd spent very little time on site. Seeing again where and how they actually lived reminded him of what a difficult existence these people actually had.

The sun had set behind the buildings and a quarter moon took its place. A single street light blinked on and off as the incandescent bulb was heated by the current passing through it. All the other street lights in the near vicinity had been shot out or were no longer working. As the night grew darker, one by one, lights from the individual apartments began to flicker on, providing little to no light for those who chose to remain hidden in the shadows.

"What now?" Vicky asked.

"It's getting late," Jake replied. "First thing tomorrow morning, we'll check with his parole officer to see if by some miracle he's shown up there. If not, perhaps Mr. Denny can give us some idea of where he might be."

The building was dark and hot. A dampness clung to Lyndsay's skin like green moss on the north side of a tree. The mattress on which she was lying sagged in the middle and smelled of rancid urine and mold. Her hands were separated and tied to the headboard and her feet to the footboard. She lay spread-eagle. Her mouth bound with a dirty, foul-tasting rag. A blindfold covered her eyes. Her lower back throbbed with excruciating pain. Salty sweat poured from her forehead and rolled into her hair. She was alone except for the sounds of the beady-eyed rats she heard scurrying above her head in the attic and along the floor.

The last thing she remembered was Terry kissing her good-bye and then leaving for his workplace. She had no idea how she had ended up in this horrible place. Her head throbbed as she tried to call out for help. She pulled at the ropes that bound her to the bed but to no avail. All she could do was pray that someone would rescue her from the nightmare. She thought of the baby inside her. She feared the stress would cause her to go into labor. She still had another month left in her pregnancy. All these things were running through her mind when suddenly, she heard someone unlocking the door. A flicker of hope that someone had come to rescue her was soon replaced by the reality of her situation.

Heavy footsteps crossed the room and stopped at the foot of the bed. Lyndsay tried to see who it was, but the blindfold prevented her from seeing anything other than total darkness. In a few moments, the person moved to the side of the bed. She could feel a slight warmth on her face. She suspected it was a flashlight. She could feel the light move up and down her body. She felt sure he was checking her bindings. She felt him lay the flashlight on the bed next to her. She cringed when she felt him lay his big heavy hand on her expanded belly. She felt the baby kick in response. After a few moments, he removed the binding from around her mouth. Her tongue searched for moisture, but there was none. She felt like she'd swallowed a wad of cotton. Without a word, he lifted her head and began pouring water into her mouth. Lyndsay hadn't realized how thirsty she actually was until she felt the cool water touch her lips. She swallowed as quickly as she could, but he was pouring the water into her mouth too fast. She began to choke. Water gushed down the side of her face, wetting her hair and soaking into the mattress. He removed the cup from her lips. When she finally stopped coughing and caught her breath, she spoke to her captor.

"What do you want from me? Who are you? What am I doing here?"

The man did not answer. Instead, he tied the dirty, sweat-soaked rag around her mouth once again, picked up the flashlight, and exited the room, locking the door behind him. Lyndsay tried desperately to call after him, but her muffled cries fell on deaf ears.

The next morning Jake and Vicky arrived at Tom Denny's office at eight sharp. Mr. Denny arrived shortly thereafter. As the detective was getting out of his car, the concerned couple approached him.

"Tom Denny?" Jake asked as he extended his hand to him.

Tom replied with a nod, a smile, and a tight-gripped handshake.

"I'm Jake Tillery and this is my wife, Vicky," Jake said, pointing to Vicky standing directly behind him.

Jake was glad when Tom released the hold he had on his hand. Jake smiled wearily and rubbed his hand to soothe the pain, hoping Tom had not intentionally inflicted on him. Wisely, Vicky did not offer her hand. Instead, she smiled and bid him a pleasant good morning.

"You two come inside. We can talk in my office," offered Mr. Denny.

When they were seated, Tom offered them coffee. Vicky declined. Jake accepted. While Tom was pouring Jake and himself a cup, Jake inquired as to whether or not Tom had seen Judas since their last conversation. Tom assured him he had not.

"What's the next step you take in circumstances like this?" Vicky asked.

"I will report his failure to appear to the police. They will put out an all-points bulletin on him. Hopefully, someone will see him, and he can be picked up. At which time, he will be sent directly back to prison."

"Vicky and I went to his apartment yesterday around six o'clock. I inquired of his whereabouts, but no one was willing to tell me anything."

Tom took a sip of his coffee and then sat the cup on his desk. "Do you need creamer or sugar?" he asked. "I don't use it, but I'm sure I could round some up for you."

Jake reached for the cup. "No thanks. Black is fine."

Tom sat down behind his desk and opened Judas's file. "I called down to the Chilton County Jail yesterday and talked to Sheriff Meed. I was hoping he could tell me if perhaps Judas had relatives living there. Sometimes, parole violators will go back to the area where they were arrested. Especially, if there is still family or friends located there."

"What did the sheriff say?" asked Jake.

"He said he didn't know of any relatives and certainly no friends. I guess the day he was arrested for killing Ginny Macon and taking her baby, the folks there were ready to lynch him on the spot."

Jake took a quick swallow of coffee then replied, "Sometimes I wonder if stringing up some of these known murderers wouldn't be such a bad idea. Especially, when there are children involved."

Tom leaned forward and laid his forearms on his desk. "You make a good point. However, when children are involved, the other prisoners don't always take kindly to child molesters and abusers. In fact, when Judas went to prison for killing Ginny Macon, he ended up with two broken arms and a scar about ten inches long across his lower back. One of the inmates cut him with a shank. He almost died. Stayed in the infirmary for right at a month."

Vicky squirmed in her chair. "Did they find Ginny's baby?" she asked.

"No," answered Tom. "No telling what became of the baby. He could have sold it on the black market, if it lived, that is. If it died, it probably ended up as buzzard bait."

Vicky's face turned pale. Tom realized that was probably not a good thing to say in her condition.

"Sorry about that," he apologized. "That was a stupid thing to say."

Vicky raised her hand. "It's okay. No harm done. I just get a little emotional these days. Things bother me that normally wouldn't."

Tom leaned back in his chair again. "Yeah, my wife gets that way when she's pregnant too."

"How many children do you have?" asked Vicky.

Tom reached for the picture sitting on the desk and turned it toward Vicky and Jake so they could see his family. "We've got seven kids in all, four boys and three girls. Number eight is due next month."

Jake and Vicky looked at the picture and then at one another. "Wow!" said Jake. "Seven kids and one on the way."

Vicky smiled, "This is only our first."

Tom sat the picture back on his desk. "Well, believe me when I say, your lives will never be the same. Children are great, but they put a whole new light on the subject of marriage."

The conversation was interrupted by the ringing of the phone.

"Excuse me," said Tom as he reached to answer it. "Hello, Tom Denny here. How can I help you?"

A panicked look came over Tom's face. "Slow down, honey," he said calmly but with a slight hint of panic. "How long has she been gone?…She probably went by the curb market for some fresh vegetables…Did you try calling the store?…Okay, Jennifer honey, just calm down. I'm sure your mom is fine, but I will call the store and ask if she is still there. If not, I'll call the curb market manager's office. Try not to worry. I'm sure she's just delayed somewhere. I'll call you as soon as I know anything."

Tom hung up the phone and reached for the local phone directory sitting on the table behind his desk. As he was thumbing through the pages, Vicky spoke.

"Is everything all right, Tom?"

Tom located the number for the grocery store where his wife always shopped. As he was dialing the number, he answered her, "That was my daughter. My wife went to the grocery store to get milk. That was over an hour ago. She hasn't returned. Probably has a flat tire or something."

The phone began ringing and a voice on the other end answered, "Good morning, Sav-A-Lot. This is Bill Headley. How may I help you?"

"Bill, this is Tom Denny."

"Oh, hello, Tom. How are you, buddy? Haven't seen you in a long time."

"I'm fine. Listen, Bill, has my wife been in the store this morning?"

"Yes, Tom, she was. I think it was around seven thirty. She bought a gallon of milk and a loaf of bread. Why?"

"My daughter called and said she hasn't arrived home yet, and she's worried. Could you look out in the parking lot and see if maybe she had a flat tire or maybe car trouble."

"Sure, Tom. Be right back."

Tom heard Bill lay the phone on his desk. He looked at Jake. "She may have run out of gas. I'm always fussing at her about needing to put gas in her car. She runs it on empty half the time."

Jake and Vicky looked at one another, knowing all too well. Vicky quite often did the same thing. They both smiled and waited quietly.

Several minutes had passed when Tom heard Bill pick up the phone again. "Tom," he said. "Her car is in the parking lot, but she is nowhere to be seen. When I saw her car, I went out and checked to see if she was in it." He paused. "Tom, her purse and the bag with the milk and bread was lying on the ground next to the car. I asked the bag boys and the cashiers if anyone had seen her, but no one has. One of the boys did say he saw an old green Volkswagen van speed out of the parking lot shortly after Tina left the store."

Tom's face became flushed. "Thanks, Bill."

"Should I call the police, Tom?"

"No, Bill. I'll take care of it. Thanks again."

Before Bill could respond, Tom hung up the phone and immediately dialed the police station. He told the operator to connect him to Detective Crawford. When the detective got on the line, Tom explained about his wife's disappearance. Before Tom had finished talking, Crawford covered the receiver, turned to Andy, and told him to put out an APB on a green VW van and also for Tina Denny.

"I am going directly home, Detective," added Tom. "My children are alone. I will take them to their grandmother's house and then I'll check out a few places I know she could possibly be."

Detective Crawford assured him he would find her. Tom knew the detective was saying that just to make him feel better, but the knot in the pit of his stomach said differently. Tom hung up the phone and looked at Jake and Vicky.

Tom stood up. "I have to find my wife," he said.

"We understand, Tom," said Jake. "We will do everything we can do to help you. I have a bad feeling that Judas Solomon may have something to do with it."

Tom closed his eyes for a split second. "I certainly hope not, Jake. But if it was him that took her, he will never see the light of day again, if I have anything to say about it."

Tom hurried out the door and was leaving the parking lot by the time Jake and Vicky got to the door of the building.

"Oh, Jake," Vicky said, her voice trembling. "I pray nothing bad has happened to that poor woman. What in the world would Tom do? I can't imagine him raising seven children alone while trying to hold down a job too."

Jake opened the door and the two of them stepped out into the sunlight. "Me either, Vick."

Lyndsay had drifted off to a nightmare-filled sleep. She was in a deep dark body of water being held down by an unknown force. She was fighting to get to the surface but was running out of breath. To her relief, she was awakened by the sound of her prison door creaking as it was being opened. Again, she hoped it was someone who had come to free her. Once again, that was not the case. She listened carefully as the man with the heavy footsteps crossed the room. Only this time, she could also sense the presence of another person. As the footsteps neared her bed, she could smell the scent of lavender, the smell a woman would use to relax, the kind she herself had used when lying in a tub of bubble bath. She could also hear breathing and the muffled sound of words struggling to be spoken.

As she listened, the man with the heavy steps passed by the foot of her bed and then stopped when he reached the other side. She heard springs creaking, presumably from another bed next to her own. She could tell the person was also being tied to the bed. She assumed it to be in much the same fashion as herself. She could hear the woman's unsuccessful attempts to get away. The heavy footed man came past her bed once again. She could feel the heat from the flashlight as he passed it along her body, checking her bindings. Soon he left the room, locking the door behind him. All that remained was the sounds of sobbing as the new inhabitant continued struggling to get free from her bondage.

If only Lyndsay could speak, she would tell her there was no use trying to get away. When the room became silent, Lyndsay groaned loudly. She wanted to let her fellow prisoner know she was not alone.

Vicky wanted to get to her office as quickly as possible in order to write an article about Tina Denny's disappearance. Two women in two days was big news. Perhaps someone reading the article had seen something, anything that might help police locate the two missing women. She had Jake drop her off in front of the newspaper building. Once out of the car, she leaned in through the open window, kissed Jake, and then quickly hurried inside.

Jake decided to go by the grocery store where Tina was last seen. Perhaps he could find out something the police hadn't. As he pulled into the parking lot, he saw one of the bag boys collecting shopping carts. Jake parked his car, got out, and called to the young man he recognized as being Brantley Majors.

"Hey, Brantley."

Brantley was a rather shy, slender-built boy in his midteens. He was trying desperately to push way too many carts for his size. He was sweating profusely, so Jake went to his rescue and began pushing the carts across the parking lot for him.

"Thanks, Mr. Tillery," he said, quite relieved.

As Jake was pushing the carts, he began questioning Brantley. "Say, Brantley, were you here this morning when Mrs. Denny was here?"

"Yes, sir. I told the police I saw her go out to her car. There was an old, half-rusted out, green Volkswagen van parked next to her car. I remember thinking how odd it was."

"Odd, how?"

"Well, Mrs. Denny's car was the only one in the parking lot. For some unknown reason, she likes to come early in the morning. And strange as it was, the van's driver had chosen to park right next to Mrs. Denny's car."

"I see. Did you notice anybody get out of the van and maybe come into the store?"

"No. I didn't see anybody, but I was busy putting up a new display for our sale on Vienna sausages. The next time I looked out, I saw the van was gone, but Mrs. Denny's car was still parked there. I thought perhaps she'd forgotten to get something and came back in the store. After that, the boss sent me out back to help unload a shipment of meat for the meat department."

By that time, Jake had reached the store with the carts. Brantley thanked him for his help and began taking the carts inside the store a few at a time.

Jake decided to go inside to talk to the store owner, Bill Headley. Jake spotted him talking to a customer near the office door. As he was walking toward the office, one of the girls working the register spoke to him.

"Hey, Mr. Tillery."

Jake looked around. It was Becky Johnson. Becky was the oldest daughter of Charlotte and Mark Johnson. The Johnson family had been homeless the first time Jake met them. They had come to the center where he worked to get help. He found them suitable housing and eventually found Mark a job with a construction firm. Becky's family was one of his success stories. Jake smiled and called out to her, "Hey, Becky. I'm fine. How are you?"

"I'm good."

"How's your folks?"

"Doing great, Mr. Tillery. Thanks to you. Dad just got promoted to supervisor."

"That's great news, Becky. Say, you didn't happen to be here this morning when Mrs. Denny was here, were you?"

"No, but I got here just as she was leaving."

"Did you notice anyone with her or someone bothering her?"

"Well, as I was getting off the bus, I saw Mrs. Denny crossing the parking lot going toward her car. She looked like she was in a hurry. When she got to her car, I couldn't see her anymore because there was this old beat-up van parked in the way. When I got to where they were parked, I looked over, and Mrs. Denny was being helped into the van by this really big guy."

"Did you see what he looked like, Becky?"

"I didn't see him real good, but I can tell you he was really big. Taller than my daddy, and he's over six feet tall. I do remember he had dark hair."

"Do you remember what he was he wearing?"

"He had on black pants and an orange plaid shirt. I remember because he looked like a scarecrow you would see at Halloween."

"Did Mrs. Denny look frightened?"

"I don't know. I couldn't see her face. She wasn't struggling or nothing. She's pregnant, so I thought maybe she was in labor, and the man was taking her to the hospital. I wish I had told somebody, Mr. Headley or Mr. Taylor. Maybe she wouldn't be missing now."

Jake could see Becky was upset. "Hey, Becky. You had no way of knowing what was going on. Try not to be upset. I'm sure we'll find her."

"Thanks, Mr. Tillery. I'll be praying for her."

"You do that, Becky. That's the best anyone can do."

Jake waited for Bill to finish his conversation with the customer before going over to him. When the rather talkative woman finally walked away, he approached Bill and stuck out his hand. Bill did the same.

"Good morning, Mr. Headley," Jake said, shaking his hand. "I'm Jake Tillery."

"Glad to meet you, Mr. Tillery."

"Please, call me Jake. I understand Tina Denny was here this morning."

"Yes, she was," Bill answered. "Do you know Tina?"

Jake reached for his business cards and handed one to Bill.

"Not really, but I have had some dealings with her husband, Tom."

Bill looked at the card he'd been handed. "Tom and Tina are nice people. They've been shopping here for as long as the store's been open."

"I'm trying to help find Tina," said Jake. "If there is anything you could tell me that would help, it would be most appreciated."

"Like I told Tom, I didn't see anything."

"Do you remember ever seeing a green Volkswagen van before today?"

Bill thought for a moment. "You know, as a matter of fact, I did see one. I had forgotten about that until you mentioned it."

"Was it here at the store?"

"Yes. It was several days ago."

"Did you see the person driving it?"

Again, Bill thought back to that day. "Come to think of it, yes I did. He was a small, thin, rugged-looking man."

"Did you see his face?"

"No. He was wearing a hat pulled low across his forehead. I noticed him because he purchased a cart full of gallon jugs of water and several large cans of pinto beans."

"Water and beans you say."

"Nothing else. Just water and beans."

"How did he pay?"

"If I remember correctly, he paid with food stamps."

Jake's mind raced. *Thin, rugged-looking man...Hat low across his face... Food assistance. Everything pointed to one person, Judas Solomon.*

Jake thanked Bill for his help and then immediately exited the store, waving a quick good-bye to Becky. When he reached his car, he opened the door and slid onto the seat. As he was about to put the key in the ignition, he noticed what looked like a flyer on the passenger's side of the car beneath his windshield wiper. Jake hated it when people left advertisements on his windshield. Now he would have to take the time to get out of the car to remove it. He stuck the key in the ignition and cranked the car. Afterward, he stepped out of the car and reached for the paper. Glancing at it, he realized it was not the average message one gets stuck on his windshield. Unfolding it, he could see the message was handwritten.

The women will be retrned once we are thrugh with em. Tell the pulice to stay off our back's or they will never be seen alife agin.

Jake's heart began racing ninety miles an hour. The handwriting, the misspelled words, the description Bill had given him, all added up again to just one person, Judas Solomon. He read the note again. *Why would he write we and our?* he thought. *Does that mean he has an accomplice? Who could the accomplice be? Someone he met in prison? A family member?* As he was climbing back into his car, he started putting two and two together. Of course he had an accomplice. The man Becky had seen helping Tina into the van. But who was he? To be sure, Jake needed to find Judas. He felt sure if he could find Judas, he would surely find the two missing women as well. But first, he needed to find Detective Crawford and make him aware of the note. As he was about to leave, he saw Brantley collecting carts again. He rolled down his car window and called to him.

"Brantley!"

Brantley turned and looked toward Jake. "Yes, sir."

"Did you see anyone messing around my car while I was inside?"

"Yes sir, Mr. Tillery," he answered back.

Jake drove over to where Brantley had collected the carts. "Did you see what he looked like?"

"He was a small, thin man with a hat pulled down low on his face."

"Did you happen to see what he was driving?"

"No. As far as I could tell, he was on foot. The last time I saw him, he was walking that way."

Brantley pointed toward the north end of the parking lot.

"Thanks, Brantley," Jake said, taking out another business card from his shirt pocket and handing it to the young freckled-faced boy. "If you see him again, give me a call. Okay?"

"Yes, sir. I sure will."

Jake pulled out of the parking lot and slowly headed north. There were several businesses along the right side of the street: Bee Bee's Laundromat, Nell's Cantina, Books and Things, and Sam's Record Shop. Out of the four, Nell's Cantina seemed to Jake as his best bet. He pulled alongside the curb and got out. The store front needed a serious paint job. There was peeling paint, as well as several pieces of rotten wood along the eaves. The large windows on either side of the double doors were covered with iron bars. Jake opened one of the doors and stepped inside.

It took a few minutes for his eyes to adjust to the sudden change of light. Once he could see clearly, he realized he was in a rather seedy-looking establishment. There were two pool tables on one side of the room, and a variety of tables and chairs, with a few of them actually matching. On the walls were pictures of Spanish women dancing in their gaily clad dresses and one of a bunch of poker playing dogs sitting around a table, holding cards in their paws, drinking beer, and smoking cigars.

Two fairly rough-looking men were sitting at the bar. One of them swiveled his bar stool around and was looking at Jake rather harshly as though he didn't appreciate his presence. The other appeared to be nursing a glass of hard liquor and could care less about who had just walked in. Behind the bar was a rather robust-looking woman with a cigarette hanging out the side of her mouth. The low-cut, tight-fitting T-shirt she was wearing exposed more of her very large breasts than Jake cared to see. Her arms looked as though she lifted weights and could very well hold her own with any number of male arm-wrestling opponents. An eagle tattoo adorned her left forearm and a fire breathing dragon bedecked her right. She smiled a half toothless grin and bid him to come on in.

Jake took a seat two stools down from the brute who was still staring at him. The barmaid placed a cocktail napkin on the bar and asked, with a rather gruff voice, what he would like to drink. Although Jake seldom drank alcohol, he ordered a light beer, paid for it with a five-dollar bill, and told her to keep the change. By doing so, he was hoping it might encourage her to give out information more freely. She smiled, winked, and placed the tip in her empty tip jar. Placing both hands on the bar, she leaned forward and began talking to him.

"Ain't seen ya in here before. My name is Carolyn Jane Roberts, but ever'body just calls me CJ. I own this here place. What's your name, handsome?"

Jake blushed.

"Jake," he answered.

"Well, Jake, what's your story? Ever'body's got a story, ya know."

"I'm looking for someone," answered Jake.

"We've heard that before. Ain't we, fellers?" she said, looking at the two men sitting at the bar. "Who might ya be lookin' fer?"

"His name is Judas Solomon. Thin fellow. Wears his hat pulled low across his face."

The sound of a glass bottle hitting the fake-granite countertop made Jake jump. The overturned beer spilled onto the counter.

Before answering, Nell picked up a well-stained rag from beneath the counter and began swabbing the countertop.

"Yeah, I know the little sorry little rat. Walked outta here without payin' fer his whiskey."

"When was that?" Jake asked, hoping it was recently.

"'Bout a week ago. Ain't seen him since. Good thang too. If I ever see 'em a'gin, I'll lay a whoopin' on him like he ain't never had before."

"Did you talk to him?"

"Some."

"He didn't happen to say where he is living now, did he?"

"Nope. Just said he was comin' into some money. Said he'd be livin' on easy street soon."

"He didn't happen to say where he was getting this money from, did he?"

"Naw, but I did overhear him talkin' to this big feller that was sittin' beside him. Something 'bout some women and their babies."

Jake's heart fell into his stomach. A knot formed in his throat. Jake laid his card on the counter and pushed it toward Nell.

"If you happen to see him again would you please give me a call?"

CJ took the card and looked at it.

"Shore 'nugh, honey, but if he comes round here ag'in, he ain't apt to be much to look at when I get through with 'im. Don't nobody fleece old Nell and git away with it."

Jake thanked Nell and left the bar. Once outside, he was glad to be breathing the fresh air again. As he was driving away, the thought kept running through his mind about the women and their babies. *Was Judas planning on selling these women's babies? Although he himself had been sold as a baby, surely that sort of thing didn't happen in this day and time.*

7

The Capture

The room was quiet now. Tina had stopped sobbing. It had been a good eight hours since Lyndsay had used the toilet. She was starting to feel like her bladder was going to burst wide open. Thankfully, she heard the sound of heavy footsteps coming to the door. She recognized them as being that of her kidnapper. Hopefully, he would allow her to go to the bathroom. She could hear the key being inserted into the lock and the door creaking loudly as it swung open. The footsteps walked across the room and stopped at the foot of her bed.

"Hey, lady," a deep voice said loudly. "Ya gotta pee?"

Lyndsay could feel the warmth from the flashlight on her face. She nodded yes. The woman next to her tried to speak, but with her mouth bound tightly, all she could do was make muffled noise.

"I'll git to ya in a minute," her kidnapper said rather angrily.

Once Lyndsay was untied, she was led to a small room with an extremely smelly toilet; one she knew she would never use under any circumstances other than the situation she was in now. Although she remained blindfolded and gagged, she attempted to point to her blindfold to try and make him understand she needed to see what she was doing.

"Forget it, lady," he said gruffly. "If I take your blindfold off and ya see me, I'd have ta kill ya when we're through with ya. Ya don't want that, do ya?"

Lyndsay shook her head no. With much difficulty, she slowly pulled down her maternity pants and squatted over the toilet she knew must be covered in filth and germs. *No way am I going to touch this nasty toilet seat*, she thought. It was extremely difficult to remain in a squatting position, but the thought of sitting on something that smelled like week-old slop in a wet knee-deep pigpen almost made her sick. Her thighs ached, but the thoughts running through her mind was enough to make her hold her crouching position until she was finished. When she was done, she pulled up her slacks and was led back to the bed where she was once again tied spread-eagle to the bed posts. Once Lyndsay was properly secured, he moved to the other bed where the other person was allowed to use the toilet also.

Lyndsay lay there thinking about what he had said. *"When we are through with you."* What did he mean by that? she wondered.

Jake was in a quandary. Should he try to get in touch with Tom Denny or Terry Cannon or just continue searching on his own? As he was trying to decide what to do next, his mind kept going back to what Nell had said back at the bar. *Did people still buy children? And what kind of person would actually buy a child?* Then he thought about his own circumstances. It was quite possible when forty years ago, his adoptive father, Wilfred Tillery, had paid for him. Sometimes good people want a baby, but for one reason or another, the system refuses to help them find one. That's when even good people will do things to get a baby they ordinarily wouldn't do. It was not those good people he worried about. It was the child abusers and molesters that concerned him.

He started thinking about Vicky and the baby she was carrying inside her. He knew Tom and Terry must feel devastated. He certainly knew how he would feel if Vicky and their baby were missing. He looked at his watch. *Surely Vick is through writing her article*, he thought. *I'll go by the newspaper office and pick her up. Then we both can decide what to do next.*

Jake pulled his car into the parking lot next to the building that housed the Birmingham News. He was about to get out of the car when he saw Vicky and her boss coming out the side door. He honked the horn. Vicky looked up, smiled, and waved. She turned and said something to Fred and then headed toward the car. Jake reached across the seat and opened the door for her. As she was getting in the car, she spoke,

"I was getting worried about you." She leaned across the seat and kissed Jake. "I was about to have Fred drive me home."

"Sorry. Time got away from me."

"Did you find out anything new?"

"Not really. I talked to the store manager. He recalled seeing a slightly built man driving a green VW van coming into the store a few days ago. He remembered him because all he purchased was a cart full of gallon jugs of water and several large cans of beans. I also talked to the owner of Nell's Cantina. She remembered him because he left without paying his tab. She also said she overheard him talking about women and their babies to a large man, younger than himself."

"Sounds like you may have made some headway to me. Have you told Detective Crawford about what you've learned?"

Jake suddenly remembered the note. He picked it up from off the dashboard and handed it to Vicky.

"I found this on my windshield when I was about to leave the grocery store parking lot."

Vicky opened the note and read it aloud.

"Jake! I don't like this one bit. Do you realize what this means?"

"What?"

"It means someone is following you, Jake. They knew you were at the grocery store. They had to be watching you."

"Yeah, I guess you're right, Vick. I hadn't thought about it that way."

"We need to get this note to Detective Crawford."

Jake put the car in reverse. "You bet."

Tina lay spread-eagle on the hard, lumpy bed. Her hands and feet remained tied to the posts. She knew she wasn't alone, which was of little comfort since the other person in the room, in all likelihood, was in the same predicament as she was. As she lay there in total darkness, she thought back to the parking lot and the man who had taken her. He had emerged from the van parked next to her. He'd done it so quickly she'd had no time to think, much less react. She looked at him, but his features were distorted by the nylon stocking he wore on his face and head. He told her to get into the van or he would kill her and her baby. She hadn't seen a weapon, but he was a big man, so she knew it wouldn't do for her to try and fight him. However, as she lay there in agony, she wished she had fought. Maybe she could have broken free.

The baby inside her moved. She felt very uncomfortable lying flat of her back. She imagined the baby must surely be uncomfortable too. It moved again. She began to pray. *Please, God, don't let my baby come now. It's not time.*

In the distance, she heard footsteps coming her way. Only this time, it sounded like two separate sets of footsteps. When they stopped, she heard the key being inserted into the lock and the door creaking as it was opened. She heard voices too. One of the voices she recognized; the other she did not. She lay as still as possible, listening to them talking to one another.

"Sit this one up first," the unfamiliar voice instructed.

Tina could hear them untying the woman next to her.

"Now tie 'er feet together and her hands too."

"How can she eat with her hands tied together?" the familiar voice asked.

"She'll figure it out," said the second one, whose voice sounded like a much older man than the first. His voice was gruff and raspy, like a person who had smoked cigarettes all his life. "Now take off her gag so she can eat. We don't want 'em starvin' to death. We need strong healthy babies."

"Should I take off her blindfold too?" asked the younger man.

"No, ya fool!" the second one yelled. "We can't let her see us! If'n she behaves herself, I might decide to let her go. Once we've got the baby that is."

Chills ran down Tina's back. *Oh my God! They're planning on taking our babies from us. So that's what this is all about. Well, they're gonna play hell taking my baby from me. I'll die before I give up my baby.*

A plate of beans was placed in Lyndsay's lap. She was also given a spoon.

The man with the raspy voice spoke to her.

"Eat up, little lady. Gotta keep up your strength."

Next to her, Tina was being untied from her bed restraints. However, unlike Lyndsay, as soon as her hands were free, she began to hit at her assailant. However, the big man struck her hard across her face. A sharp pain surged through her head like water through a burst dam. He was immediately able to take control of the situation. Once he had secured her hands in front of her and removed the gag from around her mouth, she was also given a plate of beans and a spoon. She wanted desperately to throw them in his face, but she was extremely hungry, and the fear of retaliation kept her from doing so.

As Jake was driving to the police station, he and Vicky began going over what they knew so far. "First, Jake said, "all the women he has killed, as well as the ones missing, were pregnant."

"But why?" asked Vicky. "What reason would anyone have for kidnapping only pregnant women?"

Jake thought for a moment before answering, "There can be only one logical explanation, Vick. He's taking these women so he can harvest their babies and sell them."

Vicky turned pale. "Jake! Harvest their babies? That makes it sound like babies are a product to be bought and sold."

"In the mind of the kidnappers, that's exactly what they are…an expendable item."

"Jake, we have to do something to stop him. We have to find these women and their babies before it's too late. Do you think Judas Solomon is the one responsible for these kidnappings?"

"I believe he is certainly a prime suspect. However, at his age, I don't think he's working alone. The man who forced Tina Denny into the van was a big man. Judas is nowhere near big."

Their discussion was cut short when Jake pulled up next to Detective Crawford's unmarked police car. The detective and his partner were coming out of the police station. Jake rolled down his window and called to them, "Detectives, you're just the ones we're looking for."

Jim and Andy made their way down the steps and approached the car. Jim squatted down next to it so he could see them clearly.

"Hey, Jake, Vicky. Any news?"

Vicky handed Jake the note.

Jake passed it to Jim. "I found this on my windshield as I was leaving the grocery store where Tina Denny was abducted."

Jim carefully unfolded the paper and read it aloud. When he was finished reading it, he handed it to Andy with the instructions to take it inside and give it to the lab to have it dusted for fingerprints.

"Have you made any further headway in the investigation, Detective?" asked Vicky.

"Nothing," Jim answered. "He's slick. It looks like he comes out of nowhere and then disappears the same way he came. I've put out an APB on the two women and the green VW van. We've got men checking licenses in several parts of the city, in hopes that we might get a lead that way. The mayor has made an announcement on all the local TV stations for all pregnant women not to go out alone but to travel in pairs at all times. And to report anything unusual or suspicious to local authorities."

"What do you want us to do?" asked Jake. "We want to help any way we can."

"For now, just go home and take care of Vicky. Don't let her out of your sight."

Vicky pulled out her can of pepper spray and held it up for Jim to see. "I've got my trusty pepper spray to protect me."

Jim spoke solemnly, "These men are dangerous, Vicky. They mean business. I don't think a little can of pepper spray will stop them. Best the two of you go home and let the police handle it."

Jake looked at Vicky. He could see she was tired. He knew she wanted to help as much as he did, but Jim was right.

"I think that's good advice," he said to the detective, as well as to Vicky. "It's getting late. We've done about all we can do for today."

Vicky knew Jake and the detective were right. Although she wanted desperately to find the two women, she was tired, and she hadn't eaten since early that morning. It wasn't good for her or the baby. She agreed to call it a day.

When Tina and Lyndsay finished eating, the older man told the younger one to put the gag back in Tina's mouth first. Lyndsay saw her opportunity and immediately began to speak.

"Please, mister. We promise we won't call out for help. Just please don't put the gags back on. It makes us feel like we're choking. That can't be good for our babies."

Tina shook her head in agreement and mumbled, "We promise."

There was silence. The young man spoke first.

"I don't see how it matters bout the gags no how. Can't nobody hear 'em noway. We're so far out in the sticks, ain't nobody round fer miles."

Again silence.

"Fine," said the older man. "We'll leave 'em off fer now. But if I hear even so much as a peep out of either of ya, I'll put 'em gags back on ya 'fore ya can slap a tick." He turned to the younger man. "Tie 'em back to the bed and let's get outta here. I got things to do."

When they were once again safely secured, the two men left and locked the door behind them. The two women listened as the footsteps faded. When they could no longer hear them, only then did Lyndsay attempt to speak to her fellow prisoner and only in a whisper.

"My name is Lyndsay Conners. Who are you?"

"Tina. Tina Denny."

"Oh my God. Are you Tom Denny's wife?"

"Yes. How do you know my husband?"

"I work at Social Services. I'm a social worker. Tom Denny is a parole officer for one of my clients."

A realization hit Lyndsay unexpectedly like a rock on a windshield.

"Oh my God!"

"What?"

"I knew his voice sounded familiar."

"Whose voice?"

"The older man. I know who he is."

"Who is he?"

"His name is Judas Solomon. He's on parole. He was in prison for killing a woman twenty years ago. He killed her and chopped her to pieces."

"What does he want with us?"

"I don't know for sure. I can only guess. When he killed Ginny Macon, she was pregnant. They never found the baby."

Tina began to sob. "Do you think he took her baby?"

"Well, they never found it."

"What did he do with it?"

"Again, I am only guessing, but it is likely he sold it."

"Sold it!" Tina screamed out."

"Shhhh," whispered Lyndsay. "Keep your voice down. You don't want to be gagged again, do you?"

The two women fell silent. The only sounds heard in the darkness of the damp, mildewed walls were that of quiet sobbing and several large rats as they scampered across the floor beneath the two frightened women's cots.

When Jake and Vicky arrived home, Vicky realized just how tired and hungry she really was. All she wanted to do was eat dinner, take a long warm soothing bath, get into her pajamas, lie down on her bed, read a good book, and push all the ugliness of the day aside. Since there were no leftovers in the refrigerator, Jake called the pizza shop down the road and ordered a supreme pizza with everything on it except anchovies. He then suggested to Vicky that she take that relaxing bath she so wanted, while he made a trip to the pizza shop and then to the jiffy mart to pick up a gallon of milk.

"Lock the door behind me," he said as he kissed Vicky on the cheek and headed out the door.

Vicky locked the door as she was told and immediately went to their bedroom. After relieving her bladder, she turned on the water in the claw-foot tub and adjusted the water temperature. She reached for the lavender bubble bath and poured in a generous portion. Thick white bubbles began appearing on top of the water as the gentle scent of lavender floated through the air. She looked at herself in the mirror. Her abdomen was getting bigger and bigger by the day. The baby inside her moved and a small round protrusion appeared directly under her right bosom. She laid her hand on her side and gently stroked the life within.

Vicky was lost in thought as she continued caressing her baby when she heard a noise from behind her. *Jake's back*, she thought. She looked up expecting to see Jake in the mirror. However, it wasn't Jake. Instead a huge hand clamped tightly across her mouth and her left arm was forced upward behind her back causing excruciating pain. The smell of ether filled her nostrils. In the mirror she could see a very large man with a stocking pulled over his head. As the anesthetic began working on her senses, his features became further distorted. She struggled to try and free herself but to no avail. The more she tried to get away, the further up her back he shoved her arm.

"Stop strugglin'!" he shouted. "Stop now or I'll kill you and your baby!"

Vicky's last thoughts were of the pepper spray still inside her pants pocket. Her last fleeing thoughts went back to what Detective Crawford had said. *These men are dangerous. A little can of pepper spray will do little to stop them.* He was right. Within seconds, her mind blurred, her knees crumbled, she stopped struggling, and everything around her went blank.

Jake got home with the steaming hot pizza and fresh milk. He knew Vicky liked milk with her pizza, so he took a clean glass from the cupboard and filled it with ice cold milk. He put the glass of milk, two paper plates, and the box of pizza on a serving tray and carried it upstairs to their bedroom. He walked into the room expecting to see his wife propped up on the bed with pillows behind her back, a clean body, and a renewed state of mind. Instead, he walked into the room and immediately stepped onto wet carpet.

He could hear the water still running in the bathtub. He quickly set the tray on the desk and opened the bathroom door. Water and bubbles were spilling over the edge of the tub. He waded through inch-deep water puddled on the tile floor, turned the faucets to the off position, and called to Vicky, but there was no answer. An instant feeling of panic came over him. As he was leaving the bathroom, he saw a note stuck to the condensation on the bathroom mirror. It was written with the same handwriting and misspelled words as before.

> I told ya to tell the pulice to back off. Now, I got yor purdy little wife an yor un bornd babey. Don't come lookin fer um or ya wont never see em alife agin.

Jake's heart fell into the pit of his stomach. He felt nauseated. Words of blame ran through his mind: *Why did I leave her alone? It was my fault she is gone. I should never have left her. How could I have been so stupid?*

As he walked back into the bedroom, his fear turned to anger. He saw the pizza and the glass of milk still sitting on the desk. Anger boiled up inside him like a raging river after a storm. Suddenly, he lashed out, striking the tray with a blow so hard it sent the tray and its contents flying across the room. He stood silent for a moment, staring at the pizza and the broken glass scattered across the carpet. Milk dripped down the wall and onto the carpet; the carpet Vicky picked out when they first began remodeling the house. She called the new carpet mauve. He recalled how angry she got when he jokingly called it putrid pink. A tear rolled down his cheek. He loved Vicky with all his heart. If it was Judas who had taken his wife, he had surely sealed his fate.

With trembling hands, he picked up the phone and called Detective Crawford. The phone rang twice before it was answered.

"Crawford here."

Jake's voice quivered as he told Detective Crawford what had happened.

"Stay put, Jake. I'm on my way."

Jake placed the phone back in its holder and sat down on the side of the bed. His head began to pound, and he could feel his blood pressure rising. Within minutes, blue lights from an unmarked police car stopped in front of his house. When Jake stood up, his knees wobbled. Composing himself as best he could, he made his way down the stairs to unlock the door. While doing so, a thought crossed his mind. *How did the intruder get in? Had Vicky let him in? Was it someone she knew and trusted?*

Detective Crawford and Detective Boone, along with several other officers, unknown to Jake, got out of their cars and hurried up the steps two at a time. Crawford stopped on the top step and turned to two of the men behind him.

"Check around back," he ordered two of the officers. He then turned his attention toward Jake. "Jake, do you know how he gained entrance?"

"No, Jim. I haven't checked the backdoor or the windows, but this door was locked when I got back. I know because I had to use my key to unlock it. I should never have left her alone. I was only gone for a few minutes. I went for pizza at the restaurant down the street, then stopped at the Jiffy Mart for a gallon of milk. Vicky likes milk with her pizza…" He paused. "I should have stayed with her. I could kick myself a thousand times over."

Jim laid his strong hand on Jake's shoulder. "Jake, this isn't the time for blame. We have to focus on one thing and that's getting Vicky back safe and sound."

"You're right," Jake agreed.

"Now, let's take a look upstairs."

Jake, Detective Crawford, Andy, and two men from the forensic lab ascended the stairs to Jake and Vicky's bedroom. Jake explained about the water on the floor and why there was pizza, glass and milk scattered everywhere. "I guess I just went crazy for a minute or two," he told them.

"That's understandable," replied Andy. "Was there any evidence of her having removed her clothes before being attacked?"

"No," answered Jake. "I guess she'd only just started filling the tub, and I didn't find any of her clothes amiss."

"What was she wearing?" asked Jim.

"A pair of light blue slacks, a blue striped maternity shirt, and white scandals."

Jim called out to Andy, "Call in her description and what she was wearing." He then pointed to two young officers standing just inside the door. "You two check for prints."

One of the officers who had been sent to look out back entered the room.

"Detective," he called out, directing his attention to Crawford. "We found car tracks out back. Also, the lock on the basement door that leads outside has been broken. We also found a couple of cigarette butts lying on the floor at the foot of the basement stairs."

Jake spoke up, "The cigarette butts have to belong to the kidnappers, neither one of us smoke."

The officer handed Crawford a plastic evidence bag containing the possible evidence. Crawford checked to see what brand they were. "Winstons. I'd know them anywhere. They're the same brand I smoked for years…Jake, do you know anybody who smokes Winstons?"

Jake ran all possible suspects through his mind. The only one he could come up with was Judas Solomon.

"I sure wish we could locate that sucker," Jim said angrily. "I feel sure he has something to do with these kidnappings."

"I think so too, Jim," replied Jake. "But who is the big guy witnesses have reported seeing? I mean, I know Vicky, and even though she's pregnant, she would have put up one heck of a fight."

"That's true, unless the perpetrator was holding a knife to her throat," said Andy. "He could also have threatened to kill her baby if she didn't do what he said."

Jim scratched his head. "Andy, check with the authorities at Kilby Prison. See if Judas Solomon ever had a cell mate that fits the big guy's description. If so, find out where he is.

Is he still incarcerated? If not, get ahold of his parole officer and find out where he is."

"On it, Jim," replied Andy as he headed for the unmarked patrol car.

Vicky lay in the back of the green VW van struggling to free her hands from the duct tape that bound them together. A blindfold covered her eyes. A foul-smelling rag was tied around her mouth. She tried to concentrate on things around her: the sounds, the smells, the bumps in the road. She could hear two men talking. One had a raspy voice like that of a longtime smoker. The other one sounded younger although his voice was deep and hallow. They were laughing and joking about taking her right out from under Jake's nose. There was no question in her mind these were the men who had kidnapped Tina and Lyndsay. Now they had her too. Her only hope was for Jake to somehow find her.

8

Black Market Babies

Detective Crawford got back to the station around midnight. A note on his desk said to call Allen Ewing. Ewing worked in the lab. Exhausted, Jim sat down behind his desk and dialed the lab's extension. After two rings, Allen answered the phone.

"You got something for me?" Jim asked.

"You bet. I found a partial print on one of the cigarette butts. The print matches that of Judas Solomon. He is an inmate at Kilby Prison."

"Was an inmate," Jim corrected him. "He was released on parole a few months ago."

"When are they gonna stop letting these convicted felons back on the streets? The parole board must be nuts to let a man like that go."

"I agree completely. Anyway, good job, Ewing. Now go home and get some rest."

"Sounds like you could use a little shuteye yourself."

"No rest for the weary. Thanks again. Hopefully, we can wrap this case up soon. Maybe then I can rest."

"I understand that. Good night."

"Yeah."

As soon as Allen hung up the phone, Jim put in another call. This one was to Jake, informing him about the prints. The next one went to Andy Boone.

"Did you find out anything about Solomon's cellmates?" he asked Andy.

"I talked to Warden Kirkland. The only big man that shared a cell with Solomon is still in prison. What about the cigarette butts? Anything come of that?"

Jim told his partner about the partial print matching that of Solomon. He also told him to check with Conners and Denny to see if they had heard anything from the kidnappers.

Andy was puzzled. "Do you really think this is a kidnapping for ransom, Jim?"

Jim bit at his lower lip before answering, "Honestly? No. I think this is a case of black market babies. I think these scums are planning on harvesting the babies, selling them, then killing the mothers. Black market babies are big business, one Solomon knows all too well."

"What about the earlier killings? Those women were pregnant too. Why would they kill them if they were planning on harvesting their babies?"

"Those were just trial runs. The women that were killed weren't far enough along in their pregnancy. He would've had to keep them hidden for too long unlike the three he has now. All three of these women could go into labor any minute, if they haven't already. Sometimes stress can cause a woman to go into labor early. Let's just hope we get to them in time before that happens."

Jim heard Andy yawn.

"Go home, partner, and get some sleep. We'll get started up again first thing in the morning."

"I could use a little shuteye," replied Andy as another huge yawn escaped from his mouth like a bird taking flight.

"Me too. Give my best to Sandra."

"Will do."

Jim laid the phone back on the receiver, opened the bottom drawer to his desk, took out a bottle of Jack Daniels, and poured a large portion of it into the half-empty coffee cup sitting on his desk since that morning. He took several large swallows of the strong, black, coffee-liquor mixture and then leaned back in his chair, letting the caffeine and alcohol do its work. There would be no sleep for Detective Crawford until Solomon and his elusive partner were caught and the women returned safely to their loved ones. Perhaps a trip to Kilby Prison to have a talk with Solomon's former cellmate might prove to be helpful. He would make it his first priority come morning. Shortly afterward, his head dropped onto his chest, and Detective Crawford was fast asleep.

Vicky lay quietly in the back of the green VW van. Once she realized there was no getting loose from her bonds, she began listening for familiar sounds and smells. At first the streets they were traveling on were smooth. She could hear traffic passing them on either side. *We're on the interstate*, she thought. Several minutes passed, and she could feel the van veer off to the right and down an incline. *We've taken an exit, but which exit?* There was no way for her to know. At the bottom of the incline, the van veered to the right and stopped. The driver shut off the engine and opened his door. The passenger did the same. Vicky could smell gasoline. *They've stopped to get gas. This is my chance to get someone's attention.*

Vicky rolled over on her side and began kicking the side of the van as hard as she could. The van rocked with each kick. She tried to scream, but her screams were muffled by the binding around her mouth. Seconds later the side door flew open, and one of the men jumped inside, quickly closing the door behind him. He grabbed her, pulled her away from the side of the van, and then slapped her hard across the face.

"Stop that! Are ya crazy? Don't make me have to kill ya here and now. I will, ya know," he shouted.

Vicky's face burned. Tears welled up in her eyes. Tears her capture could not see nor would he ever see. She would never let him see her cry. That was a promise she made to herself.

The driver's side door opened, and the man pumping the gas got back inside. The other man crawled back into his seat, and they were on their way. Once again, Vicky could hear cars passing by them but only on one side. *A two-lane road.* Suddenly, the strong smell of manure filled her nostrils. *The stockyards on the south end of town.* Still the van did not stop. A good thirty minutes passed.

The men sitting up front were laughing and talking. She could smell liquor. The cigarette smoke was so thick she could hardly breathe. Vicky couldn't make out all they were saying, but the one thing she could hear and understand was that these men planned on taking her baby from her. As she lay there in the back of the van, bound and gagged, she vowed to herself not to let that happen. They would have to kill her first before she would let them take her baby.

The van slowed and turned left onto a gravel road. The farther they traveled, the bumpier it became. The van made two more turns, once to the right and once to the left. Now the road was rough and treacherous. Vicky was being bounced around like a rag doll in a clothes dryer. She was thankful for the musty smelling mattress on which she was lying.

Several minutes later, the van came to a full stop and the two men exited. The side door opened, and Vicky was pulled out onto the ground. She could smell fresh air, trees, and moist earth.

"Get her inside," the older man ordered.

Vicky could feel herself being lifted off the ground. She could tell that the younger sounding man was big and exceptionally strong. She heard a door creaking as it was opened. She could feel herself being carried down a flight of stairs to another door. She heard a key being inserted into a lock. When they entered the room, she could hear the stifled voices of what seemed to her to be two other women. *The voices must be that of Lyndsay and Tina*, she thought.

She was placed on a foul-smelling mattress, rank and musty. Her hands and feet were untied only briefly before she was forced to spread-eagle, at which time her hands and feet were tied to the bed posts. She tried to speak, but the binding around her mouth smothered her words. One of the men leaned over her. She could feel his hot breath on her face. She could smell the liquor he had so recently consumed. The stench of stale cigarette smoke filled her nostrils, making her gag. She turned her head to avoid getting sick. He began laughing and grabbed Vicky's face, forcing her to face him.

"Got ya now, little lady. Let's see what your old man does to try and save his precious, darling wife. Him and his self-righteous do-gooders. Thinking they're better than anybody else." He let go of Vicky's face, stood erect, and walked to the end of her bed. "Ain't nobody can do nothin' 'cause can't nobody find ya. Don't nobody know 'bout this place 'cept me and my boy. Ain't that right, son?"

Oh my God, thought Vicky. *It is Judas Solomon, and he has a son.*

The next morning, Jake awoke to the ringing of his phone. He had fallen asleep at his desk while doing research on Judas Solomon. Drool had dripped from his open mouth onto an old newspaper article he had printed from the internet. Finally, on the fourth ring, he was awake enough to answer the phone.

"Hello," said Jake, his voice scratchy like an old 45 rpm record.

"Jake. This is Detective Crawford. Sounds like you had a rough night."

"Yeah. I guess I fell asleep here at my desk."

"I wanted to let you know we got a lead early this morning."

Jake sat back in his chair, revived by the possible good news.

"Two young men were stopped at a gas station last night at the Jemison exit. They reported seeing an older green VW bus. They noticed the vehicle because they said it sounded like someone was kicking the sides of it from the inside out. They also saw an older man fitting Solomon's description open the side door and jump inside. Afterward, the bumping sound stopped, and the VW sped away rather quickly going left on County Road 145."

"Why did they wait until this morning to report it?"

"They didn't know about Vicky's abduction until they happened to see the report on WAKA Five O'Clock News."

Jake thought for a moment. "County Road 145 takes you over to Highway 31. Right?"

"That's right. Andy is in Jemison now. He's trying to find out if anyone else happened to see the green VW."

"Has anyone talked to Sheriff Meed recently? Since he was in on Judas Solomon's arrest, I think he should know what's going on. Judas lived in and around Clanton before he was convicted of Ginny Macon's murder. Judas knows the area. It could be his holdup somewhere around Meed's jurisdiction."

"I agree, Jake. I'll put a call into his office ASAP."

Jake bid Crawford good-bye and hung up the phone. Out of pure habit, he called out to his missing wife, "Hey, Vick. Time to get up. You're gonna be late for work."

Before his words reached his ears, he realized Vicky wasn't there. He leaned forward, propped his elbows on the desk, put his head in his hands, and prayed. "Lord, help me find Vicky. She is my world. Please, don't let Judas kill her and our baby. Point me in the right direction, Lord. Give me a clue. Anything. Just don't let her or the others be dead.

Amen." Jake rose to his feet and started toward the kitchen. The phone rang, and he rushed to answer it.

"Hello."

The voice on the other end sounded faintly familiar. "Mr. Tillery, this is Sheriff Ralph Meed. I talked to you awhile back about a fellow by the name of Judas Solomon. A Detective Crawford called me and said you folks have some dead and missing pregnant women in the Birmingham area."

"Yes, Sheriff, that's right, and my wife, Vicky, is one of them."

"Sorry to hear that, Mr. Tillery."

"Please, call me Jake."

"Well, Jake, I might have some information that will interest you. Do you think you could come to Clanton?"

"If it will help me find my wife and the others, I would swim the Atlantic Ocean."

The sheriff chuckled. "Well, you might have to cross a few creeks to get here, but as far as I know, everyone of them creeks has a bridge across it."

"I'll leave right away. I should be there in about an hour and a half."

"Good deal. See you soon. Good-bye."

Jake hung up the phone. As he was looking for his keys, he spotted the cold leftover coffee in the coffeemaker. He decided he needed a shot of caffeine so he poured himself a cup, placed it in the microwave, and pushed the button for one minute. While the microwave was heating his coffee, he searched for his keys. Just as the buzzer went off on the microwave, he found them behind the loaf of bread still sitting on the counter. He thought about all the times Vicky had fussed at him for not putting the bread back in the cabinet. As he was headed out the door, he stopped just long enough to put the bread back in its place and retrieve his coffee from the microwave.

As soon as the two dreadful men left the room, Vicky began to try and loosen the gag around her mouth. She wanted desperately to find out if she was alone or if in fact the other women were there also. With much effort, Vicky managed to slip the gag out of her mouth and onto her chin; enough that she could be understood when speaking. In a whisper, she called Lyndsay's name.

"Lyndsay, is that you?"

Lyndsay responded softly, "Yes. It's me."

"I'm Jake Tillery's wife, Vicky. Is there another woman here too?"

Both women replied with a yes. Then Tina added, "I'm Tina Denny."

Vicky struggled harder to loosen her bonds. Her arms felt numb and her back hurt terribly. As she fought to free herself, she continued talking to her fellow inmates.

"We have to get out of here. Do either of you have any idea as to where we are?"

The other women responded with a no.

"I think one of the men is Judas Solomon," Vicky told them.

Lyndsay agreed, "I thought I recognized his voice."

"Don't worry," Vicky replied assuredly, "our husbands, as well as every available law official between here and the Georgia and Mississippi lines are looking for us. We'll be fine. Don't give up hope. Just pray that help will come soon."

Sometime later, as Vicky continued to struggle, the women heard footsteps. A key was placed in the lock on the door. A loud click broke the silence in the room. The door creaked as it swung open. A gruff voice called out to them.

"Time for some food, ladies. Got to keep up your strength. We need y'all to have strong healthy babies. Untie their hands, son."

The larger man went over to the first bed and untied Lyndsay's hands. She immediately began rubbing her wrists. Judas set a plate of beans beside her on the bed.

Next came Tina. She too was untied and handed a plate of food. When the big man came to Vicky, he could see her gag was off her mouth.

"Hey, Paw, this one ain't gagged no more."

Judas walked over to her bed. "I see…Well, well, Mrs. Jake Tillery," he muttered sarcastically, "aren't we the industrious one?"

"Why, Judas?" Vicky asked. "Why are you doing this to us?"

"Ain't it obvious, or are ya not as smart as I thought ya'd be?"

"Why didn't you kill us like you killed the others?"

Judas turned angry. "Cause this fool son of mine don't know his butt from a hole in the ground. He picked women who weren't far enough along in their pregnancy. The last thing I wanted to do was take care of some sorry, drug addict whore for six months. And that one from the rich side of town was on so many valium her baby might'a been born with three heads for all I know. But ya see, you ladies are a different story. I figure y'all could drop 'em babies anytime now. 'Em babies are gonna be my retirement money. Me and my boy here are gonna sell 'em babies and move to Mexico. We gonna get us a couple of purdy senoritas, buy us a bottle of tequila, and sit on the beach all day drinking margaritas and soaking up the sun. Ain't that right, son?"

The big man laughed. "That's right, Paw."

"So eat up, little ladies," he ordered. "Get 'em bellies full. We need some babies to sell."

Vicky wanted to jump off the bed and punch him right in the kisser. However, she knew that was impossible as long as they were kept secured to the bed. When they finished their beans, the big man gathered their plates and was getting ready to tie them to the bed again.

"Judas," Vicky called to him as he was about to exit the room. "Don't you know you're making a big mistake by keeping us tied up? Truth is, the more exercise we get, the sooner our babies will be born. By keeping us tied up like this, it means it will be that much longer you'll have to wait to get to Mexico."

Judas stopped just short of the door. "Maybe ya got somethin' there, little gal. Maybe ya are smart after all." He turned to his son. "Untie 'em. They ain't goin' nowhere."

"What about their blindfolds, Paw?" his son asked. "What's gonna happen if they see us?"

"Who cares if they see us," Judas jeered. "I don't plan on keepin' 'em around once't 'em babies get here. Maybe Miss Smartypants is right 'bout lettin' 'em get some exercise. Besides, they ain't going nowhere. It's pitch-black dark in this basement. Without any light, they can't even see one another."

Solomon's son untied the three women and removed their blindfolds. The women were able to remain sitting up.

Vicky wanted to get an idea of how things in the room were situated. "Can you take us to the bathroom before you go, please?"

"Can I, Paw?" the big man asked.

"Ya women shore have to pee a lot," Judas barked. "I reckon it'll be all right. Let 'em go pee."

The big man took Vicky first. The bathroom was located in the far corner of the room where they were being held captive. As Vicky was being escorted to the bathroom, she tried to take note of every detail. She counted the number of steps between the bed and the bathroom. Thirty-one. She noted that the door to the bathroom opened to the inside and the light switch was just inside the door on the wall to the left. Although the big man didn't turn on the light, she made it a point to look upward to see if there was a light bulb in the overhead socket. Vicky also wanted to establish a one-on-one connection with the big man.

"What is your name?" she asked as she stood over the commode, relieving herself.

"Why ya want'a know that fer?" he asked.

"Just curious. I can't call you son like your father does. He is your father, isn't he?"

"Yeah. He's my daddy all right."

"So your name must be something Solomon?"

"Naw. My name ain't Solomon, it's Maze. Pete Maze."

"Why don't you have your father's last name, Pete?"

"Cause before they caught him and put him in jail, he sold me to the Maze family. They was my adopted folks. James and Lucy Maze."

"Where are they now? Won't they be worried about you?"

"Naw. There're both dead. I killed 'em."

Suddenly, Judas appeared from out of nowhere. "What's goin' on in here? What's takin' ya so long?"

"She was jest askin' me some questions, Paw."

"There ain't nothin' she needs to know, what's any of her business. Now git on back in here. We got other business to attend to."

Pete took Vicky back to where the three beds were lined up against the wall. After taking the other two women to the smelly toilet, Judas and Pete exited the room, locking the door behind them. Once again the room was completely void of light.

Detective Crawford and Jake sat across the table from Percy Wyatt. Jake envied his strong muscular build although he was glad to see his massive hands bound with handcuffs. A strand of dark greasy hair hung over his left eye. Detective Crawford spoke first.

"I understand you were a cellmate of Judas Solomon."

Percy sat slump-shouldered in a straight-backed metal chair. He crossed his right leg over his left knee. His prison-issued black-and-white striped pants rose upward on his leg, revealing a mass of dark leg hair. "Yeah. So?" he answered bluntly.

"Did Judas ever talk about himself? Where he came from, or perhaps where he lived before he was sent to prison?" asked Detective Crawford.

"He was from somewhere up north." He paused. "Say, what's this all about? Has he done got in trouble again?"

Detective Crawford leaned forward, placing his elbows on the table in front of him. "Right now, we just want to ask him some questions about some missing women."

Percy laughed. "Missin' women ya say? That don't surprise me none. He hated women. He said the only thing they was good for was havin' babies. Ain't none of 'em women pregnant, are they?"

Jake quickly answered first. "All of them, including my wife."

Detective Crawford continued his questioning. "Did he say why he hated women?"

"Yeah," Percy answered. "He said his mama was a whore and a drug addict. He said when he was five years old, his old lady started swappin' him for drugs. Men would come to where they lived, wake him up in the middle of the night, and have sex with him while she watched, drugged out of her mind."

"I see," said Detective Crawford. "How did he get down here?"

"He said when he was around eleven, he decided to run away. He hopped a train and ended up in Nashville, Tennessee. He was picked up for shoplifting food from a corner market and was put in juvenile detention. From there he went from one foster family to another until he ran away again and ended up in Montgomery. He met a feller by the name of Bruce somebody. I can't remember his last name. Together, they began kidnapping and selling babies on the black market."

"Did he ever talk about some place close where he might have stayed or lived?" asked Detective Crawford.

"Naw, not that I remember…but then I do remember he said he worked one time at a slaughterhouse near Clanton. He lived in the basement."

"Did he say where the slaughterhouse was in Clanton?" asked Jake.

"Naw, just that it was way back in the woods near a pig farm."

Detective Crawford rose to his feet. Jake did the same.

"Thanks for your help, Percy," said the detective. "I'll make sure you get an extra twenty bucks in your account at the prison store."

Percy uncrossed his legs and leaned forward. "Thanks. And by the way, I hope ya catch old Judas. I never liked him in the first place. Don't care much for a man who'd rape a woman, then sell his own baby after he killed its mama."

The detective and Jake started to walk away, when suddenly, they both stopped and looked directly at one another. It was as if, out of the blue, they both realized what Percy had just said. Both of them turned around to face him. Detective Crawford put both hands on the table and leaned forward.

"Are you saying Judas had a child?"

"Yep. He told me he raped some woman named Ginny somethin'. Nine months later, he went back to her house, killed her, and cut the baby from her womb. He then sold the baby to some people by the name of Haze or Maze, something like that. They named the little baby boy Pete. When Pete turned eighteen, Judas began writing to him. Pete used to write him back. Judas always said he was gonna look his son up if he ever got outta here."

"Did you ever see Pete?" asked Jake.

"Just before Judas was released, Pete came to visit with him."

"Can you tell us what he looked like?" asked Crawford.

"He was a big boy. Didn't look nothin' like his paw 'cept for his eyes. Both of them had dark-colored eyes, almost black. Their eyes reminded me of shark's eyes, blank with no soul, no feeling in 'em."

Detective Crawford extended his hand to Percy. Percy did the same. They shook hands and bid the other good-bye. Percy had given them the information they needed to move forward with the case, and for that, Crawford was grateful. As he and Jake left the prison, Crawford felt confident that they would soon find the three missing women. His only hope was that they would find them in time before Judas had a chance to kill them and take their babies.

9

The Escape

Now that Vicky, Lyndsay, and Tina were free to roam around the darkened room, Vicky felt perhaps they had a chance to get away. However, moving around in total darkness was almost impossible. She decided to try finding the bathroom to see if the light in there actually worked. To find the bathroom, she would have to try and retrace her steps. She recalled the number of steps it took to get to the bathroom. Slowly and carefully, she took one step at a time, counting as she went.

"One, two, three, four, five, six, seven, eight…"

She stumbled on something laying in the middle of the floor and almost fell. Regaining her balance, she reached down and picked it up. It felt like a pair of pliers. She decided to put it in her pocket. With her hands out in front of her, she once again began to count her steps. "Nine, ten, eleven…"

When she had counted to twenty-nine, she reached her arms out as far as they would go. "Thirty…" Her hand touched something solid. It was cold and rough. She felt sure it was the wall. Since she wasn't sure where along the wall she was, she decided to go left. She felt along the wall. Her face touched something sticky, a spider web. Vicky hated spiders. She quickly pulled the web from her face and continued onward until she came to the corner of the room. She thought about going back the other way until she remembered the bathroom was near the corner of the room. A few feet from the corner wall was a door. She found the doorknob and turned it. It opened. Carefully, she stepped inside and felt along the wall for the light switch. When she located the switch, she flipped it upward and a dust-covered light bulb flickered to life.

Lyndsay and Tina were overjoyed and instantly began clapping. Vicky quickly stuck her head out the door to quiet them. "Shhhhh. We don't want them to know what we've found."

Lyndsay and Tina sat side by side on the edge of the first bed and held each other close, trying to contain their excitement. Vicky looked for something, anything she could use to subdue their captors. In the dimly lit corner of the bathroom, behind the commode, she saw a tall can covered in cobwebs and dust. She leaned forward, bracing herself on the back of the commode. When she pulled the can from its hiding place and wiped away a quarter inch of dust, she could see it was a can of wasp spray. She shook it to see if there was anything inside. She could feel the liquid moving back and forth. *This will make an excellent weapon*, she thought. *If it will kill a wasp, surely it will burn a man's eyes.*

After another quick search of the bathroom, the only thing she found was a half-used roll of toilet paper. Although it couldn't be used as a weapon, it would keep them from having to drip dry every time they urinated. She thought about leaving it on the edge of the nasty sink but promptly decided against it. Instead, she pulled up her blouse and placed it between her belly and the waistband of her pants. As she started out the door, she reached into her pocket to get the pliers she'd stepped on while searching for the bathroom. In doing so, she felt something else in her pocket. She pulled it out. It was a Bic lighter. She had completely forgotten about it. She remembered having picked it up while sitting at Fred's desk doing research. She must have inadvertently put it into her pocket without thinking. *I'll never fuss at Fred for smoking ever again*, she thought. How they would go about getting the upper hand on their kidnappers was yet to be seen, but at least they had a chance now.

After leaving the prison, Detective Crawford and Jake decided to pay Sheriff Meed a visit. Perhaps he could tell them where to find the abandoned pig farm. They arrived in Clanton around ten in the morning. As they were entering the courthouse building, Jake spotted the man he recognized as Sheriff Meed. He called out to him.

"Sheriff. Can we have a word with you?"

Sheriff Meed walked over to where the two men stood. Jake reminded the sheriff of their last encounter. It had been when Jake was looking to get information about the death of Sudie Hubert.

"Yes, I remember you," said the sheriff.

Jake shook the sheriff's hand and then introduced him to Detective Crawford. The sheriff invited the two men to join him in his office. The room was small but adequate. The sheriff took a seat behind his green metal desk. Jake and Detective Crawford reached for two metal chairs that were leaned against the wall, unfolded them, and sat down across from the sheriff's cluttered desk.

"Sorry about that. I should've got those for you. So what can I do for you, fellers?" asked the sheriff.

Jake spoke first. "We need information about an abandoned pig farm somewhere around these parts. You wouldn't happen to know where it is located, would you?"

The sheriff leaned back in his chair and rubbed his chin with his thumb and forefinger. "I do recall a farm like that. A couple by the names of James and Lucy Maze owned the farm. Tragic situation."

Detective Crawford leaned forward and rested his elbows on his knees, his hands clasped together in front of him. "Tragic, how?" he asked.

"Well, you see, they were both killed," answered the sheriff. "Their son, Pete, found them in one of the hog pens torn to shreds. Folks figured they was pouring the contents of the slop bucket into the feed trough, lost their balance, and fell in. I never was completely convinced of that notion. However, since there was little evidence to prove otherwise, I had to let it go."

"What happened to the boy?" asked Jake.

"Well, he never was quite right in the head. He pretty much isolated himself from the town folks. Some of the churches around the area carried food out to him for a while. He never would come to the door, so they would just leave the food on the porch. When they would go back to take more food, the last food they delivered would be gone, leaving nothing but the empty containers. About a year after James's and Lucy's demise, the main barn caught fire and burned to the ground. No one ever saw Pete again."

"Did he die in the fire?" asked Jake.

"Well, we never found any evidence of that. No body, no bones, nothing. Same as it was when James and Lucy got Pete. One day he wasn't there, and the next day he was. James and Lucy never told anybody where he came from. It was obvious James and Lucy were not his real parents. He didn't look a thing like either of them. Some folks said Lucy couldn't have children, so the couple bought him from one of those black market baby rings."

"Can you show us where the farm is?" asked Detective Crawford.

The sheriff looked at his watch. "I'll be glad to, but first I have to testify at a wife beating case. In fact, that is where I should be right now. Why don't you fellers go across the street and down the block to the little cafe. Miss Patsy makes the best apple pie you ever put in your mouth. I'll join you as soon as I'm done in court."

The three men stood up, shook hands, and walked out of the sheriff's office. Sheriff Meed headed down the long hallway to where court was in session. Jake and Detective Crawford made their way out of the building, crossed the street, walked the half block to Patsy's Kitchen, and walked inside. A bell above the door signaled their entrance. The room fell silent. Every eye in the cafe was focused on the two strangers. Jake and Detective Crawford nodded their heads, found an empty table near the window, and took a seat.

A young blonde-haired girl, who looked to be in her early twenties, approached their table with two glasses of ice water and two menus. She smiled politely and set the glasses down in front of them. Next, she handed them a menu. "My name is Sheila. I'll be your waitress. What can I get you fellers to drink?"

Detective Crawford smiled back and asked for a cup of coffee and a piece of apple pie. Jake said he would have the same. Sheila collected the menus and then headed back to the counter to get their order.

"I always feel strange when I'm in a small town," said Jake.

"Do you mean because of the looks we're getting?" Detective Crawford chuckled.

"Yeah. You'd think we're aliens by the way they're looking at us."

"They're just being cautious. I'm from a small town south of here. You ever heard of Ramer, Alabama?"

"Yeah. I've been through there a couple of times on my way to visit Vicky's family."

As soon as the word Vicky came out of Jake's mouth, his stomach rolled over, and he literally felt sick. *How can I be sitting here having coffee and apple pie when Vicky is somewhere out there going through who knows what?* he thought. He looked across the table at Detective Crawford.

"Jim, we have to find Vicky and the others. If something happens to her, I don't think I can stand it."

Jim assured him they would find the three missing women and that everything would work out fine. He tried to sound positive even though he wasn't.

Sheila returned to the table with their order. She set a large piece of pie and a hot cup of coffee in front of each of them. "Will there be anything else?" she asked.

"No," answered Detective Crawford. "This is fine. Thank you."

Detective Crawford immediately picked up his fork and began eating. Jake stared at his piece of pie for several minutes, but he couldn't bring himself to try it. All he could think about was how much Vicky loved apple pie. Her mother always made one special when she knew he and Vicky would be coming for a visit. He finally pushed the pie aside and took a drink of coffee instead. Detective Crawford finished his slice rather quickly.

"Are you gonna eat that?" the detective said, pointing to Jake's piece of pie.

Jake pushed the pie across the table. "No. I don't feel much like eating. Help yourself."

Just as Detective Crawford was finishing his last bite of Jake's pie, the bell over the door clanged loudly. The two men looked up. It was Sheriff Meed. Jake motioned for the sheriff to join them. When the sheriff reached the table, he noticed the empty pie plates.

"Didn't I tell you Miss Patsy makes the best apple pie south of the Mason-Dixon line?"

Detective Crawford wiped the crumbs from around his mouth and smiled. "It was good all right."

Sheila hurried over to the table and put her arm around the sheriff's waist. "Hey, Uncle Ralph."

Sheriff Meed smiled. "Hey, honey pot. How's my favorite little niece?"

"Great," she answered. "What can I get you, Uncle Ralph? How 'bout a piece of Miss Patsy's apple pie?" She looked at Jake and Detective Crawford. "When it comes to eatin' apple pie, Uncle Ralph is Miss Patsy's biggest fan."

Sheriff Meed lovingly squeezed Sheila's shoulders. "I'll have to pass on the pie for the time being. These gentlemen and I have some investigating to do...Say, Sheila, has there been any strange-looking characters through here lately?"

Sheila giggled. "Ya mean stranger than the ones that usually come through here?"

Detective Crawford reached into his jacket pocket and pulled out a picture of Judas Solomon and handed it to Sheila.

"This is one of the fellows we're looking for. He might have been with another fellow, younger but bigger."

Sheila took the picture and looked it over carefully.

"Ya know, there is a guy who comes in here ever so often who looks like this picture. In fact, he was in here yesterday." Sheila walked over to the counter and held up the picture for Miss Patsy and Roscoe, the cook, to see. "Isn't this the guy that ordered five specials to go, then sat down and ate one of them here?"

Patsy reached for her reading glasses hanging around her neck and put them on. After studying the photograph for several minutes, she removed her glasses from the bridge of her nose and looked at Sheila. "Yeah. That's him all right. Squirrelly looking feller. Ate every bit of food on his plate, then complained that the food wasn't fit to eat."

"Did you notice what kind of vehicle he was driving, or which way he went when he left here?" asked Detective Crawford.

"I did," answered Sheila. "He was driving some kinda old green-looking van. I think it had a big silver VW on the front of it. What made me notice was how he sped out of the lot throwing gravel everywhere. I thought it was strange to see a man his age driving like that."

"Which way did he go?" asked Sheriff Meed.

Sheila pointed south. "He went that-away."

Jake and Detective Crawford stood up. Jake laid a twenty-dollar bill on the table. "Thanks, Sheila," Jake said.

Sheila picked up the twenty. "I'll get your change."

"No. You keep the change," said Jake.

Sheila looked at the twenty in her hand and smiled. "Thanks, mister."

Detective Crawford took a card from his pocket and handed it to Sheila. If he comes in here again, I'd appreciate it if you would call us immediately."

"Better yet," added Sheriff Meed, "call me. I can be here faster than two shakes of a Billy goat's tail."

Sheila grinned and gave her uncle a hug. "I will, Uncle Ralph."

The three men walked out of the cafe and stood beside the sheriff's car.

"What now?" asked Jake.

"How about I show y'all where that old pig farm used to be?"

"Sounds like a good idea. You go ahead. We'll follow you," said Detective Crawford.

Vicky turned off the light in the bathroom, flicked on the Bic lighter, and carefully made her way back to where the other two women were sitting on the edge of the first bed. When the two women saw the lighter, they were surprised.

"Where did that lighter come from?" asked Tina.

"It was in my pocket. I didn't even know it was there. I must have picked it up when I was at the newspaper office. I also found a pair of pliers and a can of wasp spray."

"What good will those things do?" Lyndsay asked reluctantly.

"I'm not sure just yet," answered Vicky. "But for now, it's all we've got."

Tina groaned.

"What's the matter?" asked Vicky.

"I've been having severe pains in my lower back. I think I might be going into labor."

Lyndsay gasped. "Oh no! Not now for God's sake!"

Vicky tried to keep a level head. "We have to find a way to get out of here."

Tina groaned again.

"Lay back on the bed, Tina," said Vicky. "Try to relax and keep as quiet as you can. If the baby is coming, there is nothing we can do to stop it. We may have to deliver it ourselves."

"What!" shouted Lyndsay. "We can't deliver a baby here!"

"Shhh," Vicky urged. "We can if we have to. The important thing is not to let our kidnappers know the baby is coming. She flicked the lighter again and held it close to her watch. It was approaching three o'clock. "They won't be coming back with our dinner until around five or six. We have to figure out a way to get out of here before then."

Tina laid down on the bed. "But how?" she asked.

Before Vicky could answer, Tina felt a gush of water, which quickly soaked into the mattress. Lyndsay shifted her seating position on the bed. When she did so, she felt something stick her in her buttocks.

"Ouch!" she said loudly.

"Shhh," warned Vicky again. "You have to be quiet."

"Something stabbed me in the butt," Lyndsay complained.

"Stand up and let me see," said Vicky.

Lyndsay stood up. Vicky flicked the lighter on again and felt along the edge of the bed where Lyndsay had been sitting. Something sharp pierced her finger. She looked closer. "It's a spring. One of the springs has broken through the mattress."

Vicky thought for a moment. "That's it! If I can break off a piece of the wire spring, maybe I can use it to pick the lock on the door."

"Do you really think you could do that?" Tina asked with a brief moment of hope.

"I don't know for sure, but I can certainly try."

Vicky pulled the pliers from her pocket. "Hold the mattress up, Lyndsay."

Lyndsay lifted the edge of the mattress and quickly realized it was wet. "Why is the mattress wet?" she asked.

"My water broke," answered Tina.

"Oh my gosh!" wailed Lyndsay. "What are we gonna do now? You can't have the baby now!"

Vicky looked up from her project. "The first thing we're going to do is remain calm," she told Lyndsay. "So hold up the mattress and let me work on getting a piece of wire."

At first, she tried using the pliers to cut the piece of wire, but it was too thick and she wasn't strong enough. She decided then to clamp the pliers onto the wire and maneuver it back and forth, hoping the wire would eventually break. After several minutes, the spring gave way, and she was able to retrieve a section of wire just long enough to fit into the keyhole.

In the meantime, Tina's contractions were getting closer and closer together.

"We have to hurry," Lyndsay said in a panic. "The baby appears to have moved downward into the birth canal. Do something, Vicky!"

Vicky handed Lyndsay the lighter and then sat down on the foot of Tina's bed. "Okay, Tina," she said firmly, "this baby can't wait any longer. Raise your legs and spread them as far apart as you can. Lyndsay, get closer with that lighter."

Both women did as they were told. Tina pulled her feet toward her body until her heels almost touched her buttocks. As soon as she spread her legs apart, Vicky saw the baby's head. *Thank God I took those birthing classes when I was in college*, she thought. Sweat popped out across her forehead. *Hopefully, I can remember what to do.*

"Okay. Here we go, Tina. Now push!"

Tina grabbed the edges of the mattress with both hands, drew in a deep breath, and, with one ear-piercing scream, pushed as hard as she could. Within seconds, a new life was born.

"It's a boy!" said Vicky triumphantly.

Sheriff Meed turned off the main road onto what appeared to be a long deserted gravel road. Years of neglect had left the narrow road rutted and washed out in places. Low hanging branches from the towering trees on either side of the road formed a darkened tunnel. As he carefully made his way down the abandoned lane, Spanish moss slid across the top of his patrol car like fingers caressing a lover. Although the journey was tricky to maneuver, the sheriff noticed the pathway appeared to have been traveled recently. There were fresh tire tracks going in and back out again. Halfway down the road, a dispatch came in on his car radio.

"Sheriff, this is Dot."

Sheriff Meed picked up the mic. "Yeah, Dot. This is me."

"Sheriff, I just got a call from your niece, Sheila. She says one of them men y'all are looking for just came into the cafe."

"Ten-four, Dot. Did she say which one it was?"

"Naw. But she did say he was a big feller."

"Thanks, Dot."

"Yes sir, Sheriff."

Sheriff Meed stopped his patrol car, got out, and hurried back to the car behind him. Detective Crawford rolled down his window. "What's up, Sheriff?"

"One of them men is at the cafe. I think it's Pete. Sheila told Dot he was the big one. What y'all want to do?"

The detective looked at Jake. "What do you think, Jake?"

Jake thought for a moment. "Something tells me we need to check out the pig farm. Sheriff, how about you go back to the cafe and see what you can find out? We'll go on ahead."

Sheriff Meed agreed. "I think there's a turnaround just ahead. Y'all wait until I turn up in there, then y'all just go straight ahead down this road. It'll take you right to the pig farm."

The sheriff got back into his car. A little ways down the washed-out road was a side road. The sheriff turned his patrol car onto it and waited for the detective's car to go past. As soon as the other car got past the turnoff, the sheriff waved his hand out the window and headed back to the main road.

A mile or so down the dirt road, the two men saw a clearing up ahead.

"That must be the pig farm," said Jake.

Detective Crawford brought the car to a halt in front of what appeared to be an old abandoned farmhouse. The wood siding was cracked and void of paint. The tin roof was rusted and curled up in places. The two men got out to investigate. As they were nearing the front steps, Jake noticed dried, muddy footprints going up the steps.

"Look, Detective," Jake pointed out. "Those footprints appear to have been made recently."

Detective Crawford reached inside his jacket, located his shoulder holster, and pulled out his gun. As quietly as possible, they ascended the dilapidated steps. When they reached the rundown porch, the floor creaked loudly with every step they made. A gruff, raspy voice from inside the house called out to them.

"Is that you, son?"

The two men looked at one another. Detective Crawford decided to answer.

"Yeah. It's me, Dad."

Immediately, they heard a crashing sound as though a chair had fallen over. Next came what sounded like the slamming of the back door. Detective Crawford crashed through the front door and into the front room of the house. There was a small table and two chairs sitting next to the back wall. One of the chairs was toppled over on its side. On the table was a half-empty bottle of whiskey, two dirty glasses, and an empty box from Fowl-Mouth Fried Chicken House. Detective Crawford called out to Jake.

"They must have…" he stopped in the middle of his sentence when he realized Jake was not behind him.

Alarmed, he called out, "Jake!"

When Jake heard the back door slam, he immediately headed around to the back of the house. Just as he rounded the end of the house, an old blue pickup truck came tearing across the yard like it had been shot from a cannon. The truck headed straight for Jake at breakneck speed. Just before the truck got to him, Jake was able to jump onto the back porch, avoiding a collision with the speeding vehicle.

Detective Crawford rushed out the front door as the truck went speeding past. The man driving looked straight at him, shot him a bird, and began laughing. The detective took aim and fired at the truck's tires but missed. The truck quickly sped away in a cloud of dust.

"Jake!" Detective Crawford yelled again. "Are you all right?"

Jake came around the side of the house in a full run. "Did you get him?" he yelled.

"No! I missed!"

"It was Judas Solomon. I saw his face plain as day."

"Yeah, I know. I saw him too. Get in the car, quick. We'll go after him."

Jake hesitated.

"You go, Detective. Something tells me I need to stay here and look around."

Detective Crawford jumped off the edge of the porch and headed for his car. "You look around. I'll see if I can catch up to the pickup."

As soon as the detective was gone from sight, Jake headed for one of the dilapidated buildings. Once inside, he could smell the rancid odor of rotting flesh and pig manure. As he inspected the stalls, he saw the skeletal remains of what appeared to be a large sow and ten small piglets. On one side of the barn was a small room. Jake opened the door. Inside were sacks of decayed, half-eaten pig feed. Several large hairy rats scampered across the floor, disappearing through a hole in the wall. In the loft above were stacks of old hay turned moldy and mildewed. An old tractor was parked in one of the stalls at the back of the building, its tires dry rot and flat, its gears rusted.

Behind that barn was another shotgun-style barn. It was long and wide with stalls on either side of a narrow walkway. Jake imagined it as a working pig farm with swine of all sizes and gender. He could almost hear the haunting squeals of the chosen pigs being pulled from their stalls to face the slaughterhouse. When he reached the back of the barn, he saw still another building. There were cement steps going up to what appeared to be a loading ramp. Jake assumed this was where the pig carcasses were loaded into ice trucks and shipped away to be butchered and sold.

He walked up the steps onto the cement deck and peered inside. Large hooks hung from the ceiling like crooked icicles formed by a blowing wind. Below was a cement pit stained with blood that once dripped from the slaughtered swine. A drain in the middle of the pit held stagnate water and rotted mulch. Jake was about to leave the slaughterhouse when he noticed a closed door in the corner toward the back of the room. He decided to check it out too.

The heavy metal door creaked loudly as he pulled it open. There was total darkness. The only light Jake had on him was a small flashlight that was attached to his car key ring. The only time he used it was to unlock the driver door when getting into his car at night. It gave off limited light and certainly not enough to illuminate an entire room. He clicked on the tiny light. Cement steps descended into total darkness. Jake decided he would go back to the old house to look for a lantern or at least a bigger flashlight. He was about to leave when he heard what sounded like a muffled scream.

Vicky wrapped the newborn baby in a piece of cloth torn from one of the sheets. She used the roll of toilet paper to clean away the blood and mucus from his face and nose, then handed him to Tina. Now that the baby was delivered and appeared to be doing well under the circumstances, her biggest fear was if their kidnappers had heard Tina scream. She needed to get all of them out of there as quickly as possible. She looked at Lyndsay, who looked as though she was in shock. Vicky gently touched her arm. Lyndsay jumped.

"Lyndsay," Vicky said softly as not to alarm her. "Bring the lighter over here to the door. We've got to get out of here before those men come back, or they'll take Tina's baby."

The two women made their way across the dark room, leaving Tina to comfort her newborn baby. Vicky retrieved the piece of wire from her pocket. Lyndsay flicked on the lighter and held it close to the lock. Vicky inserted it into the keyhole and began twisting it back and forth. After several minutes, she felt the lock click. She looked at Lyndsay and smiled. "I think we did it."

Lyndsay replied, "No, you did it."

Just as Vicky was about to turn the doorknob, they heard steps coming toward them. "Oh my God," Vicky whispered. "Someone's coming. Quick! Get back to your bed!"

Detective Crawford sped down the long narrow lane, hitting every rut and bump at breakneck speed. It felt as though his teeth were being jarred right out of his head. At first, he could barely see the red taillights from the pickup. However, as he got closer, his headlights engulfed the truck. He knew it was Judas, and he knew he was dangerous. He reached for his radio and quickly made contact with the sheriff.

"This is Detective Crawford!" he called out, his voice trembling from the adrenaline rushing through his body. "I am in close pursuit of the suspect, Judas Solomon. We are coming up on Highway 31 near the old pig farm. I will need your men to set up a road block as soon as I find out which way he goes on 31. Do you copy?"

The radio crackled.

"Ten-four," answered Sheriff Meed.

The sheriff alerted his deputies to be on standby.

Up ahead, the blue pickup turned left onto Highway 31 headed south toward Mountain Creek and Marbury. Detective Crawford did the same.

"Set up a road block at the intersection of 31 and County Road 20," he called out to Sheriff Meed. The sheriff passed along the information to his deputies.

Within minutes, two county patrol cars and a state trooper car formed a blockade at the designated intersection. Some of the locals who had heard about the chase on their police monitor raced to the scene and were parked in the parking lot at the corner store.

"We ain't had this much excitement in Marbury since Bubba ran his front-end loader through the car wash and nearly tore it down!" yelled one of the anxious onlookers.

In the distance, the siren on Detective Crawford's car could be heard drawing closer to the intersection. As the siren got louder, blue flashing lights appeared in the distance. Excitement rose as the deputies and the state trooper took their positions behind their cars, their pistols drawn. Sheriff Meed reached the blocked intersection just in time to hear the sound of screeching tires. To the officer's dismay, the truck made an unexpected left-hand turn onto County Road 63. Sheriff Meed grabbed his radio, pushed the talk button, and yelled into the receiver.

"Ya idiots! He's turned down 63! Why didn't ya'll block that road too?"

Before the other officers had a chance to answer, he yelled at them again. "He's headed for 143! One of ya'll get to the end of east 20. The other one get down 31 to 143. We'll block him in. I'll hit 63 and get in behind Crawford."

The deputies jumped into their cars and headed for their assigned destinations. The trooper put in a call to the Autauga County Sheriff's Department.

"We're in pursuit of an older blue pickup truck. The truck is believed to be driven by the kidnapper or possibly the kidnappers of the three missing women. I am requesting assistance from your department since we are dealing with the borderline between both Chilton and Autauga counties."

The Autauga County dispatcher received the request and immediately called for their officers to aid in the pursuit.

Halfway down sixty-three was a railroad track. Judas's truck was nearing the tracks. He could tell by the sound of the whistle the train was just around the bend. He smiled and then pressed the gas pedal down to the floor. The truck backfired and lurched forward, crossing the tracks just short of being hit by the speeding train. The conductor blew his whistle loudly as his train rumbled past County Road 63.

Detective Crawford slammed on his brakes and came to a screeching halt. Angrily, he pounded his fist on the steering wheel before reaching for the radio. "I've lost him. I got caught by the train."

His radio crackled again. "So did we," one of the deputies called from his position at the end of County Road 20E. All they could do was sit and wait until the train passed before resuming their pursuit.

At the end of County Road 63, Judas turned right onto 143 headed toward Elmore County. He was thrilled. Once again he had eluded the law. Once again he was still a free man.

When Jake neared the end of the long, dark hallway, he saw a door. *I wonder if it's locked*, he thought. *Only one way to find out.* Cautiously, he reached for the knob, slowly turned it to the right, and pulled. To his surprise, it was unlocked. As he pulled it open, it creaked loudly. He peeked inside the darkened room. With the tiny penlight, he could only see a few feet ahead of him. He stepped into the room. He could smell a strange odor. A moment later, Tina's baby began crying unexpectedly. Jake almost jumped out of his skin.

"Get back!" a voice yelled at him. "I have a weapon!"

It took Jake a moment to comprehend the situation. *Could the voice actually be that of Vicky? It sounded like Vicky.* He called out to her, "Vick, is that you?"

Lyndsay flicked on the lighter. There in the darkness, Jake saw the face of his beautiful wife for the first time in three days. She was holding what appeared to be a spray can aimed directly at him. Beside her was Lyndsay holding a flickering lighter. Seated on the bed was Tina. In her arms was a baby. Without another moment's hesitation, Jake ran to his wife and threw his arms around her. Vicky did the same. Relieved, they all began smiling and laughing. They were safe at last.

When the train finally passed, both the sheriff and Detective Crawford continued their pursuit. Unfortunately, the blue truck had completely disappeared. Every paved road, dirt road, and pig trail was searched but with no luck. Eventually, the truck was located in the next county near the little town of Slapout. However, Judas was nowhere to be seen. Sheriff Meed sent word to Will Deason, the constable over in Billingsley, about bringing his hounds to help track Judas down. He knew Will had some of the best tracking dogs in the state.

Shortly after dawn, Will arrived in Slapout with three of the finest, biggest, red bloodhounds the sheriff had ever seen. As soon as Will stopped his truck, the hounds were ready to go. One-by-one, Will attached a lead rope to their collars before letting them out of the carrier. Once they were on the ground, Will took them to the abandoned pickup so they could get a whiff of the escapee. The lead dog, Max, jumped directly onto the seat and began sniffing everything in the cab. Bo and Lilly sniffed the ground around the truck. Upon command, all three dogs headed due west through the woods. Will could tell they were hot on his trail by their low, woebegone baying.

10

Happy Fathers

Jake, Vicky, Lyndsay, Tina, and her new baby made their way down the long, dark hallway. They were just short of the stairway that led to their freedom when they heard footsteps coming from above. They all froze dead in their tracks. Vicky grabbed Jake's arm.

"They're back!" she whispered in near panic.

Jake released the button on his penlight. The hallway went completely dark.

"Stay calm, everyone," Jake replied as quietly as possible. "Do you still have that spray can?"

"No," Vicky answered. "I left it back there."

Jake knew the can of wasp spray was their only weapon. He would have to go back and get it. "Stay here and keep quiet," he told the others.

"Don't leave us, Jake," Vicky pleaded.

"I have to, Vick. I have to get the spray can."

Jake could not turn on his penlight for fear that whoever was at the top of the stairs would see it. He made his way back to the room where the women had been held captive by feeling along the damp wall with his hand. When he got to the end of the hall, he bumped his head on the door. It creaked loudly. Jake prayed no one had heard it. Once inside, he turned on the penlight and quickly surveyed the room. There at the foot of the bed lay the can of wasp spray. Jake hurried over and picked it up. The can was rusty and covered in dust, but it was their only means of defense. Once he had it in his hand, he rushed back to the hallway and followed it back to the frightened women by the same means as before.

Above them, the women could hear the sound of pots rattling and plates being loaded onto a tray. They knew one or both of the men were preparing to feed them. Jake had not returned yet, and they were very afraid. *What if they were captured again? The men would take Tina's baby from her. They might beat them or maybe even kill them for trying to get away.* Those were the thoughts running through the women's minds.

Suddenly, there was a light at the top of the stairs. The three women huddled close to the wall. Tina held her tiny infant close to her bosom. Step-by-step, he descended the stairs. Without warning, the baby began to cry. The person on the stairs dropped the tray, sending food, plates, cups, and eating utensils cascading down the stairway. Tina tried to quiet her baby, but it was too late. The damage was done. Within seconds, Pete was at the bottom of the stairs with a huge flashlight. He pointed it directly at them, blinding the women.

"What the?" he yelled at them. "How did y'all get out? Is that a baby I hear?"

Pete came at them, wide-eyed, like a madman. He immediately grabbed for the baby, but Tina refused to relinquish her child. Lyndsay and Vicky began hitting Pete on the back and across his arms. Tina whirled around with her back to him and pressed her precious baby as close to her as she possibly could without smothering him. She was determined she was not going to give up her baby to this madman.

Jake came within fifteen feet of Pete without being detected. He pushed the switch on the mini flashlight to the on position, lifted the can of wasp spray, and pointed the nozzle directly at Pete's glaring eyes. He pushed the button, but nothing happened. He released it and then pushed it again. Still nothing. *The nozzle must be stopped up*, he thought. He hurriedly scraped at the pinhole with his fingernail, pointed it once again directly at Pete's eyes, and pushed the button again.

At first, there was little more than a drizzle shooting a few feet out in front of him. Pete heard the hissing noise the spray can was making. He lifted his flashlight and shined it in the direction of the noise. For the first time, Pete realized the three women were not alone. He was looking directly into the face of Jake Tillery. For a split second, their eyes met. In the next second, the nozzle came unplugged and a stream of wasp spray shot out the end of the nozzle directly into Pete's eyes. Immediately, he dropped the flashlight and began rubbing at his eyes, wailing.

"Run!" Jake yelled. "Get out of here!"

Tina and Lyndsay headed up the stairs.

"I'm not leaving without you!" Vicky yelled back as she reached for the flashlight lying on the floor in front of her. She lifted the long-handled flashlight over her head with both hands and with one solid blow, brought Pete to his knees. She hit him a second time directly on the top of his head, and he went down with a thud. Blood trickled from a cut on the back of his head. Jake jumped over his body, and he and Vicky rushed up the stairs, leaving Pete passed out cold as a cucumber on the damp musty floor.

When they got to the top of the stairs, Jake found a length of steel pipe lying on the floor near the blood pit. First, he locked the door leading down the steps, then he put the pipe through the handle for good measure. He wanted to make sure Pete wasn't going anywhere. Pete was now a prisoner of his own making.

As soon as the three of them were safely outside, Jake took off his denim jacket and handed it to Tina. She removed the dirty cloth from around her baby's body and replaced it with the jacket.

"Do the three of you want to wait here while I go to the main road to flag down a passing motorist?" Jake asked the women.

"No way!" they responded in unison.

Jake put his arm around Vicky's shoulder. "Well, all right then," he replied. "Follow me."

When they reached the main road, the sun was beginning to peak over the horizon. Hues of bright orange, red, and yellow mingled brilliantly with the scattered, low hanging clouds. Just as they started walking south down Highway 31, Jake saw a welcome sight. It was Detective Crawford's unmarked patrol car. A huge smile crossed his face as he waved his arm high above his head. The detective pulled up beside them and rolled down his window.

"You folks need a ride?" he joked.

The dogs stayed hot on the trail of Judas for close to an hour. Unfortunately, the search was brought to a screeching halt just east of the Elmore and Autauga County line. The sheriff concluded that someone must have been waiting there to pick him up, or he hitched a ride with an unsuspecting motorist. Either way, Judas Solomon had once again avoided being captured.

Sheriff Meed watched as Will put Max, Lilly, and Bo back into their carrier. He was not at all happy about the situation. "I can't believe we lost him again," he said to Will. "It just beats all I've ever seen. He's either the smartest or the luckiest felon I've ever seen in all my years in law enforcement."

Will closed the door on the wooden box that held his three dogs. All three of them were worn to a frazzle. They immediately laid down inside the carrier to rest. "Ya got that right," Will agreed. "He's a slick one all right. Have ya heard if Jake had any luck at the pig farm?"

The sheriff had almost forgotten about Jake. He was just getting ready to put a call in to the dispatcher when a voice came over the radio in his car.

"Sheriff, this is Carolyn. Do you copy?"

The sheriff picked up the receiver. "This is Sheriff Meed. Go ahead, Carolyn."

"Sheriff, I just got a call from Detective Crawford. Jake found the women. They were being held captive in the basement of the old slaughterhouse. Everyone is safe. They're on their way to Prattville General Hospital by ambulance. Tina Denny had her baby only minutes before Jake found them. And Sheriff, Detective Crawford said you could find Pete locked up in the old slaughterhouse there at the pig farm. He says he'll meet you there."

"Well, glory be!" exclaimed the sheriff. "That is good news. Call Terry Cannon and Tom Denny if you ain't already. I know they'll be glad to know their wives have been found and are safe."

"Ten-four, Sheriff. I'll get right on it. Do you want one of the deputies to meet you at the slaughterhouse?"

"That won't be necessary, Carolyn. Will Deason is here with me. I'll get him to help me bring him in."

"What about Judas Solomon? Did y'all find him yet?"

"No, I'm sorry to say we didn't. The trail ended on the road next to the Confederate Cemetery. I suspect he caught a ride with somebody. Let's just hope he don't kill 'em once he's through with 'em."

"That's a big ten-four. See you back at the station, Sheriff. Y'all be careful arresting that Pete fellow. I hear he's a big'un."

"Will do, Carolyn. Thanks for the heads up."

As soon as the sheriff got off the radio, he asked Will to go with him to the old slaughterhouse so they could bring in Pete. Will agreed to help. Shortly afterward, they headed for the pig farm.

When the sheriff and Will arrived at the pig farm, another less pleasant surprise awaited them. The sheriff drove his squad car around the barn with the intentions of parking alongside the slaughterhouse. Will followed close behind. They were both anxious to locate and arrest Pete in hopes that he might tell them where to find Judas. However, as Sheriff Meed was getting out of his car, he noticed what appeared to be someone's legs laying on the ground near the far side of the cement loading dock. To be on the safe side, he removed his revolver from his holster and carefully made his way toward the body. When he reached the corner of the dock, he could see it was Daniel Robinson.

Mr. Robinson owned a small country store off County Road 143 and was well liked and respected in the community. He was lying face down. There was a large gash on the back of his head. Sheriff Meed called out his name, but there was no response. He leaned over and put his index finger on his neck to check for a pulse. There was none. Will walked up behind him.

"Is he still alive?"

"It don't appear so. I can't feel a pulse. Help me turn him over."

The two men turned over Mr. Robinson's body. His lips were purple and there were no signs of life.

"Doggone it," said the sheriff. "Chances are, Mr. Robinson is the one who picked up Judas Solomon. I was afraid this was going to happen and it did. I just hope he didn't find Pete."

The two men rushed up the steps and entered the slaughterhouse with their guns drawn. There was no sign of anyone. "The door to the basement is over here," said Sheriff Meed.

As they approached the door, they could see it was no longer locked as Detective Crawford had said it was. The two men were about to descend the steps when they heard several cars pulling into the yard. Will looked out the window. "It's Crawford and Boone."

The sheriff and Will decided to wait until the other law officers came inside before going down into the basement. They were hoping they would not only find Pete, but also Judas. Crawford and Boone entered the slaughterhouse holding two large flashlights. As Detective Crawford approached, he stuck out his hand to the sheriff. The four of them shook hands.

"I see Judas struck again," said Crawford.

"Yeah," answered Sheriff Meed. "It's sad. Mr. Robinson was a nice feller."

"I don't expect to find either Pete or Judas in the basement," said Crawford. "I suspect they're long gone by now. I wanted to arrest Pete as soon as I knew where he was being held, but I didn't want to leave Jake and the three ladies on the side of the road to wait for the ambulance. Since Tina had just had her baby, I thought it best to get her to the hospital as quickly as possible. I really thought for sure he'd be safely tucked away until I returned."

As soon as Tom Denny and Terry Cannon heard about the rescue of their beloved wives, they immediately left Birmingham and headed for Prattville General Hospital. After a two-hour trip, Tom was soon reunited with Tina and his newborn son they aptly named Jake Victor Denny after his rescuers, Jake and Vicky. Terry, on the other hand, had to wait in the delivery waiting room for three hours before being reunited with Lyndsay, as she was busy giving birth to a big fat baby girl they named Victoria Anne.

While everyone involved celebrated the return of their loved ones, Jake and Vicky made a visit to the hospital cafeteria. As they walked down the food line, Vicky asked for some of everything except the beans. She told Jake she never wanted to see another pinto bean as long as she lived. Both of them took a seat next to one another and ate like there was no tomorrow. Just as they were finishing their meal, Dawson, Beth, Mama Cora, and Kayleen walked through the cafeteria door. As soon as Kayleen saw the two of them, she made a mad dash to where they were seated and began hugging Vicky as tightly as she could.

"We were so, so worried about you, Vick," she stammered. "Are you okay?"

Vicky laughed at her enthusiasm.

"I'm fine," she answered. "Just full as a tick right now."

After hugs and kisses, everyone sat around the table talking about what had taken place over the past few days.

Dawson began by apologizing for not being there to help look for Vicky and the others. "I was on the road when Beth called. I was just south of Butte, Montana. As soon as I dropped off my load in Great Falls, I drove straight through to get back here. It took me all of two and a half days."

Jake and Vicky assured him they were not upset with him.

"There was nothing you could have done, Dad," assured Jake. "Every law enforcement officer between here and the state line was on the lookout for Solomon."

Mama Cora patted Vicky on the hand. "Well, at least my babies are safe and that awful man is in jail."

"He's not in jail, Mama Cora," Jake replied.

Mama Cora was stunned. "What do ya mean he ain't in jail?"

"They're still trying to find him. As far as I know, they have his son, Pete—"

Dawson stopped Jake.

"His son?" he asked, quite surprised.

Jake explained the situation to his family.

Mama Cora ran her fingers through her hair. "Well, if that don't beat all I ever heard told."

Vicky smiled and leaned forward to kiss her husband's grandmother when suddenly, she felt something warm and wet puddling up in her chair and running down her legs. A surprised look came over her face. She looked at Jake and then back to Mama Cora.

"I think my water just broke."

"What!" Jake shouted.

Vicky looked down as water dripped from the chair onto the floor. A sharp pain hit her in her lower back and the muscles in her lower body contracted.

"I think it's time, everyone," she announced.

Jake ran out into the hallway and grabbed a wheelchair he'd seen there as they had entered the cafeteria earlier. When he got back to the table where his pregnant wife was still seated, he helped her into the chair and quickly headed for the delivery room. The rest of the family followed close behind.

"Don't worry, Vick," called Beth, "you're gonna be fine. Nothing to it."

"Mom," scolded Kayleen, "she's having a baby. No way can you honestly say there's nothing to it."

"I just mean women do it every day," replied Beth.

Vicky looked back over her shoulder. "Listen. If Tina Denny can have a baby in a pitch-black room with no one to help except two other terrified pregnant women, then I think surely I can do it in a hospital delivery room with both nurses and an experienced doctor standing by."

When Jake reached the doors going into the delivery room, a middle-aged nurse dressed in green scrubs took control of the situation. She directed Jake and the others to have a seat in the waiting room and then wheeled Vicky through the automated doors and began preparing her for the coming of the baby.

While they were waiting, Tom and Terry came to the waiting room and invited them to come and see their new babies through the nursery window. Everyone gathered around the window. Soon the curtains were drawn back and there among several other newborns were Victoria and

Little Jake. Ohhhs and ahhhhs passed among them. Tom passed out cigars covered in blue shiny paper that read It's a Boy. Terry did the same; only his were pink and read It's a Girl.

Just before it was time to close the curtain, the nurse who escorted Vicky into the delivery room came into the nursery holding a bundle in her arms. Her face was covered in a white paper mask. When she saw Jake and the others, she made a quick detour to the window and pulled back the blanket covering Baby Tillery's face. Beneath the blanket was a round-faced, fat, rosy-cheeked baby. The nurse pointed to Jake and then to the baby.

Jake beamed with joy. "Mine!" he yelled loudly.

The nurse nodded her head yes.

Jake held up the blue and pink cigars, one in each hand. The nurse pointed to the blue one.

"A boy!" Jake yelled even louder than before.

Once again the nurse nodded yes.

Jake began jumping around like a wild banshee. Everyone was congratulating one another when another nurse came from the delivery room holding another bundle. Mama Cora noticed it first.

"Someone else has had a baby at about the same time as ours," she informed them.

That nurse also came over to the window. Jake began looking around to see where the father of this baby was, but there was no one there. The second nurse pointed to Jake and then at the baby she held in her arms. Jake's mouth dropped open. He pointed at the baby and then at himself. The second nurse nodded yes. Jake's knees began to tremble. For the second time, he held up the two cigars. That time, the nurse pointed at the pink one.

This time it was Kayleen who began jumping for joy. "We've got twins!" she shouted. "A boy and a girl!"

Jake felt as if he was about to faint. "Oh my goodness," he exclaimed. "I can't believe it. The doctor never said a word about twins. What are we going to do? We have only one baby bed, only one highchair, only one of everything."

"We can fix that," Dawson assured him.

"What about Vicky?" Jake asked. "Is my wife okay?"

Both nurses nodded yes simultaneously.

Testosterone flooded the hallway of Prattville General Hospital like a tsunami in spring. All three new fathers were like little kids in a candy shop. Even Dawson felt giddy at the thought of being a new grandfather, especially to twins. When viewing time was over, one of the nurses came over and closed the curtain. All three fathers watched their new babies as long as the closing curtain allowed. Within minutes, Dr. Till, the doctor who delivered the three babies, came through the delivery room doors and walked over to where the family was still gathered near the nursery window.

"I'm assuming you fellows are the proud fathers," Dr. Till stated.

Jake offered his hand first, introducing himself and the others as well. Dr. Till shook hands with each of them.

"Sorry, I haven't been out to give any of you a report, but your wives have kept me rather busy," said Dr. Till. "Everyone is fine. Your wives asked to be in the same room so they are being moved to a ward. The babies are healthy and all is well."

"When can we hold the babies, Doc?" Jake asked.

Dr. Till smiled.

"As soon as the ladies are settled in their room, the nurses will bring the babies to them. You will each need to wear a sterile gown and a mask, but I don't see any reason why you can't see and hold the newborns at that time."

Jake smiled, thanked Dr. Till, and blissfully shook his hand for a second time.

Before returning to the delivery room, Dr. Till instructed the families to wait in the waiting room until the nurse came to get them. Tom and Terry had not eaten since early that morning so they decided to check out the Dairy Queen just down the road from the hospital. Jake's family gathered in the waiting room. Dawson excused himself, saying he would be back shortly. While they were waiting, a volunteer pink lady entered the room.

"Is there a Jake Tillery in here?" she asked.

Jake stood up.

"I'm Jake Tillery."

"There is a long distance phone call for you at the front desk, Mr. Tillery."

Jake followed the young girl to the lobby. When they approached the desk, the receptionist handed Jake the phone. Curious as to who would be calling him at the hospital, Jake put the receiver to his ear.

"Hello. This is Jake Tillery."

"Jake. This is Jim Crawford. Is everything okay down your way?"

Jake was happy to hear Jim's voice. "Everything is great, Jim. Tom and Tina have a new baby boy. Terry and Lyndsay have a new baby girl. And would you believe, Vicky and I have twins, a boy and a girl?"

"Well, well. Now ain't that something? Congratulations. Glad to hear everyone is safe and doing well."

"Thanks, Jim. I suppose our kidnappers are safely secured in jail."

There was a slight pause. "I'm afraid not, Jake."

"What?" Jake asked, both surprised and leery.

"Judas eluded us. We had every cop in the area after him. He dumped the truck he was driving and hitched a ride with a local elderly man. When we went back to the pig farm to get Pete, we found the old man dead. It appeared he was hit over the head with a tire tool."

"What about Pete? You got Pete, didn't you?"

"I'm sorry to say, Pete was gone too. Judas somehow circled back to the pig farm and rescued him before we could get there to get him. Judas is one slick puppy all right."

Jake could hardly believe what he was hearing.

"What next?"

"I've ask the local police to put an officer outside Vicky's, Tina's, and Lyndsay's room. They should be there soon."

"The girls requested they be put together in one room."

"Even better. I'll let the captain know only one officer will be needed."

Jake was stunned.

"Do you really think that is necessary, Jim?"

"I certainly hope not, Jake. But when you're dealing with a man like Judas Solomon, you can't take chances."

"I guess you're right, Jim. Better to be on the safe side."

"Well, I better go for now. I need to get busy trying to find these two crazy people. Give my regards to Vicky. Keep her safe. After all, she is the best reporter the Birmingham News has."

"I will, Jim. Thanks for calling. Keep us informed."

"Will do."

Just as Jake was hanging up the phone, three uniformed police officers entered the lobby. At the same time, Dawson came walking up too.

"What are they doing here, Jake?" Dawson asked.

"I'll tell you in a minute, Dad."

Jake walked over to the officers and explained to them about the change in accommodations for the three women. They decided among themselves as to who would take the first shift. The officer who remained introduced himself as Officer Norman Ewing. Arrangements were made with the front desk to provide Officer Ewing with a chair that would be placed outside room 211. When everything was finalized, Jake and Dawson headed back toward the waiting area. Dawson handed Jake a bag.

"I thought you might want to hand a few of these out yourself," he said to Jake.

Jake opened the bag to reveal a box of cigars. On the top of the box was a picture of the cigars inside. On one half of the cigar was blue paper. On the other half was pink paper. The writing across the middle read It's a Boy and a Girl.

Jake smiled.

"Thanks, Dad."

Dawson could tell something was bothering his son.

"What's goin' on, Jake? Ya look worried."

"I just got a call from Detective Crawford. He's the detective who's been in charge of this case from the beginning. He called to tell me that Judas Solomon and his son, Pete, eluded the cops and got away. Not only that, they killed an old man in the process."

Dawson felt the anger building up inside him. "What kinda cops y'all got in Birmingham anyway? How could they let them escape? Is that what the Prattville cop is for, to stand guard over Vicky and her friends?"

"Yes, Dad. Jim says it's just a precaution."

"Surely to God them fools wouldn't try to steal the babies from the hospital…would they? Are they that dumb?"

"I wouldn't say dumb, Dad. Desperate maybe."

"Well, I can promise you this, son. They'll never get their stinking hands on any of the women or our babies. Not as long as I'm alive. I've had one baby taken from me, but I can tell ya now…there won't be another."

With that, Dawson turned and headed back toward the lobby.

Jake called after him.

"Dad, where are you going?"

"I'm gonna find Judas Solomon and his mentally deranged son. And when I do, I'll put an end to all their meanness."

"Dad!" Jake called out. "You can't…"

Dawson stopped, turned, and looked back at his son with a stern look of determination. "I can, Jake…and I will."

With that, Dawson disappeared around the corner and was out the front doors in a flash.

Jake was in a tizzy as to what to do next. He wanted to stay with his wife and new babies. But on the other hand, a part of him wanted to go with his father. He wanted to see the felons stopped. He wanted to see them get their just punishment. As he was turning over in his mind exactly what he should do next, Kayleen came running down the hallway.

"Uncle Jake," she called out to him. "They have Vicky and the others in their room now, and the babies too. The nurse said we can see them now. Hurry! I can hardy wait to hold them."

As Kayleen approached her uncle, she could see he looked distressed.

"What's the matter, Uncle Jake? Is something wrong?"

Jake didn't know if he should alarm the others by telling them about Judas's and Pete's escape. He felt as though Vicky and the others had been through enough already. He decided to keep it to himself for the time being. He smiled and took Kayleen by the hand.

"Let's go start spoiling those babies," he joked.

As Kayleen and Jake were making their way toward room 211, Kayleen inquired as to the whereabouts of her grandfather.

"I know he is dying to hold his new grandbabies," she noted.

Jake hated lying to his niece, but he hated telling her the truth even more.

"He had some errands to run. He'll be back soon," he lied.

However, when they reached room 211, Officer Ewing was already stationed outside the door.

"Why is a policeman sitting outside Vicky's room?" she asked.

Before Jake could answer, the young officer tipped his hat to Kayleen and answered for him.

"It's just a precaution, miss. Nothing to worry about."

Jake was glad he didn't have to lie to Kayleen a second time. It appeared she accepted the young man's answer. Her attention immediately went back to holding her new baby cousins.

Dawson was determined to keep his promise to stop Judas and Pete. When he reached his truck, he slid onto the driver's seat, took out his keys, reached across the cab, and unlocked the glove box. Inside it was a holster that held his .38 caliber, snub-nosed, Smith & Wesson. He took it out of the compartment, checked to make sure it was fully loaded, laid it on the seat beside him, put the keys in the ignition, and started the engine. After putting the truck in reverse, he sped out of the parking lot and made a left-hand turn onto Highway 31 headed north toward Mountain Creek.

As Dawson made his way toward his destination, events from forty years past flooded his mind like a dark raging river. The long-ago, thought-to-be forgotten details of Sudie's murder were as real as the day it happened. The smell of his dead wife's blood seeped into his nostrils like a snake slithering through wet grass. The taste of iron lay heavy on his tongue like a slow-melting peppermint drop. He felt the same sinking feeling in the pit of his stomach as he did the night the sheriff told him she was dead and practically accused him of her murder. He remembered going back to the scene of the crime days later when the thought of the horrific way she had met her demise made him sick to his stomach. As all those memories tore at the very core of his being, another thought suddenly flashed across his mind. *Is it possible that Judas Solomon is the one who had not only raped and killed Ginny Macon and kidnapped his precious daughter-in-law, but was also the one who had killed my beloved Sudie? Surely not*, he thought.

It was nearly one o'clock in the morning and pitch-black dark by the time he got to the Marbury turnoff. Up ahead he saw flashing blue lights from a patrol car. The closer he got to the lights, it became quite clear he was approaching a road block at the intersection of Highway 31 and County Road 20. It had been years since he'd been back to his old stomping grounds. He wasn't even sure who the present sheriff in Autauga County was anymore. Although he had a permit to carry a gun, he quickly decided it was best they didn't discover the revolver that lay next to him. He picked it up and slid it beneath the seat.

Two deputies stood beside their patrol car. One of them waved a flashlight back and forth, motioning Dawson to stop. Dawson slowed and then came to a rolling stop next to the young man in a uniform. The deputy motioned for Dawson to roll down his window. Dawson gladly abided.

"Good evening, sir," the young man said. "I'm Deputy Dalton Stewart. May I see your license and registration please?"

Dawson put his truck in park, took his wallet from his back pocket, opened it, and took out his license. Next, he opened the glove compartment and removed the registration. He was glad he had removed the gun from inside it. After slamming the glove box shut, he handed both documents to the deputy. While Deputy Stewart went back to the patrol car to run a check on the vehicle, the second officer began a conversation with Dawson.

"Sorry about the delay, mister," he apologized. "I'm Deputy Max Carson. We are looking for two fugitives believed to be in this area."

"Is that right?" Dawson replied.

"Yes, sir. And they're armed and dangerous."

"You don't say?"

Deputy Stewart came back to the truck and handed Dawson back his information.

"Everything checks out okay, Mr. Hubert."

Dawson began putting his license back inside his billfold.

"Say, young man," Dawson inquired. "Who's the sheriff now around these parts?"

"That would be Sheriff Ralph Meed," Deputy Carson answered.

"Well, sir," Dawson replied. "Young Ralph made sheriff, did he?"

The two young deputies looked at one another with a rather puzzled look on their faces. Dawson went on to explain his reaction.

"I knew Ralph Meed when he was no older than the two of you. He helped investigate the murder of my wife, Sudie Hubert."

"Say," said Deputy Stewart, "I've heard the sheriff mention that case. It was his first murder investigation. Something about the woman being pregnant, but they never found the baby. Didn't they arrest your aunt for the murder or something like that?"

"Yes," answered Dawson. "She spent most of her life in a mental institution. However, she wasn't the one who killed Sudie. It's a long story. One I really don't have time to get into."

"Yeah, sure. We understand." said Deputy Carson.

Feeling bad about having to cut the deputies off short, Dawson added one last comment. "The only other possible suspect was a transient known only by the name of Silas."

Again, the two young officers looked at each other rather strangely.

"Hang on a second, Mr. Hubert," said Deputy Stewart.

In a few seconds, the deputy returned to the truck with some paperwork in his hand. He then began thumbing through it while Deputy Carson held up a flashlight so he could see what he was looking for. Suddenly, Deputy Stewart smiled and tapped the paper in his hand with his forefinger.

"I thought so," he said excitedly. "Judas Solomon's middle name is Silas. Judas Silas Solomon."

"Wow!" said Deputy Carson. "You don't suppose he could be the same person who killed your wife. That was like forty years ago."

Dawson was in shock. His hands began to tremble and a huge lump formed in his throat. *Dear, God*, he thought. *Is it possible after all these years Sudie's killer could finally be apprehended?*

"We need to call this information into the sheriff," said Deputy Carson.

"Yeah, well, I need to be on my way too," said Dawson.

The two young officers bid Dawson good-night and waved him on his way.

As Dawson was pulling away, he began talking to himself. "Okay, Dawson. Think. If you were a fugitive from the law, where would you hide out?" Without any reasonable answer to his own question, he drove down one road after another. There was no sign of the two men he was searching for. Truth was, he didn't know the two men he was looking for or even what they looked like. All he knew was he had to find them to try and put a stop to their crime spree.

Vicky, Tina, and Lyndsay were clearly exhausted after all they'd been through over the past few days. The husbands and close family members had taken more than their fair share of pictures of the newborns. Mama Cora wisely suggested they all leave and let the women get some rest. With final hugs and kisses, the room soon fell silent. The three women said their good-nights to one another and quickly fell asleep; their babies safe within the confines of the hospital.

By the time everyone was outside across the street from the hospital, the sun was peeping over the store tops like a mischievous youngster peeking in a bakery shop window. At that moment, Mama Cora, Beth, and Kayleen realized Dawson was nowhere to be seen. Jake told them what his father had said about finding and stopping Judas and Pete. Mama Cora was deeply concerned.

"Oh my Lord, Jake!" she said, grabbing Jake's arm. "Ya can't let him do this. Ya got to find him. He'll kill them boys as shore as I'm standin' here. Then he'll go to prison for the rest of his life."

Beth agreed. "We have to find him, Jake, before he does something stupid."

Kayleen began to cry. "What if those horrible men kill him first? I know Papa is tough, but there's two of them and only one of Papa."

Jake put his arms around Kayleen's and Mama Cora's shoulder and hugged them close.

"Don't worry," he assured them. "Dad will be fine. I'll find him and bring him home in two shakes of a Billy goats tail. Do y'all have a way to get home?"

"I have my car," Beth answered.

"Good," said Jake. "Y'all go home and get some sleep. I'll find Dad."

"Do be careful, Jake," warned Mama Cora. "You're a daddy now. I don't know what Vicky and them babies would do without ya. I don't know what we would do without ya either."

Jake kissed Mama Cora on the forehead and smiled.

"Don't worry. I'll be fine and so will Dad. Besides, the police may have already captured the fugitives by now. They're probably locked away in a jail cell somewhere."

Jake didn't know if he was trying to convince the women or himself about his father's safety. What he did know was he needed to find Dawson to make sure his father was safe, not only for the women, but also for himself. As soon as the women were on their way back to Montgomery, Jake headed north toward Mountain Creek.

11

Searching the Roads

The entire night, Dawson searched every road between Marbury and Mountain Creek. It was nearing dawn when, without realizing it, he turned onto the dirt road that ran past the house where he and Sudie had lived when she was murdered. Somehow the road seemed narrower than it had when he was a younger man. The farms that once thrived along the roadside were now nothing more than thick underbrush and leafless trees. Low hanging limbs brushed the top of his truck as he eased his way down the winding gravel road. As he rounded a sharp curve in the road, he realized he had come upon the old house he once called home. He was shocked to see it was still standing. It was almost hidden from view by tall weeds and an overgrown hedgerow. Jake pulled off to the right side of the road and stopped the truck. He was about to get out to have a look around when he noticed what appeared to be tire tracks leading into the woods about a hundred yards or so down the road.

Could be hunters, he thought. *Better to be safe than sorry though.* Dawson hesitated for only a moment before reaching under his seat to retrieve his gun. He made sure the safety was on before tucking it into the back waistband of his Levi's jeans. Slowly and cautiously, he made his way toward the house through the thick broom straw and weeds.

The tin roof that covered the house and had once lulled Dawson, Sudie, and Baby Beth off to sleep with the steady fall of raindrops tapping out a steady and methodical rhythm was now rusty and curled up in places. The steps leading onto the narrow porch had rotted and collapsed. The porch had several missing boards. Others were broken in half with one-half still hanging on by a single rusted nail and the other half rotting away on the ground below. The screen door clung to its casing like a young child clinging to its mama's coattail, held there by a single rusty hinge. One of the cedar tree columns that held up the roof of the porch had fallen, allowing the north end of the porch to dip down. Despite the dilapidated ruins, something inside him made him venture forward.

Stepping on the floor joists, which appeared to still be in decent shape, Dawson made his way to the door on the left. The doorknob was missing, so Dawson pushed the door open and stepped inside. To his shock and amazement, the furniture he and Sudie had moved into the house some forty years ago was still there in the room, untouched. The bottom drawer of the chifforobe was open just as it had been on the day of Sudie's murder. The clothes she was going to wear to her baby shower were still laid out on the mildewed bedding.

"Unbelievable," he said to himself.

A raspy voice from behind him made Dawson jump.

"It is unbelievable, ain't it?" the man's voice asked.

Dawson whirled around and immediately reached for his gun.

"I wouldn't do that if I were you, mister," the man warned. "Ya see, my son, Pete, over there in the corner don't take kindly to havin' folks pointin' a gun at his pappy."

Although it was rather dark in the house, Dawson could see the figure of a very large man standing in the corner, holding what appeared to be a very large gun.

"Who are you?" Dawson asked, his voice trembling.

The raspy-voiced man pushed the door closed before answering.

"I think it best ya give me that gun ya got tucked away before I answer any questions ya might have."

Dawson reached for the gun.

"Be careful now," said the man. "Don't get no ideas 'bout bein' no hero. Take out the gun slow and easy and throw it on the floor."

Dawson did as he was told.

"Good man. Now how 'bout we go there in the kitchen and have a seat?"

Dawson crossed the room and stepped through the opening, which led into the kitchen. A red sun had just begun to peak the horizon. Through the broken kitchen window, Dawson could see hues of red, orange, yellow, purple, and lavender streaking across the sky. He remembered how Sudie enjoyed standing at that same window, holding Beth tightly in her arms, watching the sun come up together.

"Sit!" ordered the raspy-voiced man.

Dawson pulled one of straight-back chairs from beneath the dust-covered table and sat down. He could hardly believe what he was seeing. It was as though everything in the house remained frozen in time: The coffeepot sitting on the iron cook stove. The biscuit pan, rusted and warped. The box of lighter wood against the back wall. In his mind's eye, he could see Sudie the morning before her death: her belly filled with the baby growing inside her, preparing his breakfast, talking about how she was so ready for the baby to come, not knowing she would never live to see her precious child.

The scraping sound of the other chair being pulled across the wooden kitchen floor brought Dawson back to his present situation. As the gruff-voiced man sat down across from him, he came face-to-face with his wife's killer, Judas Silas Solomon. He could feel the fire of anger and contempt, which had laid dormant for many years, rekindling inside him. He wanted to end the vile life that sat before him. He wanted him to pay for all the years he'd missed out on watching his son grow up, the sleepless nights he'd spent standing at his bedroom window longing for his murdered wife, and thinking about what horrible things had taken place that ended her life.

"So ya found me," Judas said, smiling wickedly. "Good job. Better than that half-baked sheriff and his bunch."

Dawson stared straight into the dark lifeless eyes of the evil before him.

"Why?" he asked simply.

"Why?" Judas repeated sarcastically. "Why not?"

"I know my wife. She would'a given ya food if ya was hungry. Ya didn't have to kill her."

Judas threw his right arm over the back of the chair, crossed his leg in front of him, and sneered.

"Yeah, ya know your wife all right. She was more than willing to give me a biscuit and a hot cup of coffee. It was good too. But ya see, I didn't come here fer no biscuit. I come here to get that baby she was carrying. I'd been watching her for some time. She was ripe. I knowed it was time to harvest that little seed. Old man Tillery was happy to pay me two hundred dollars fer a strong healthy baby boy. I 'pect he would'a paid twice that had I asked fer it. But a deal is a deal, and I stuck to my end of the bargain."

Dawson could feel his face turning red as his blood pressure began to rise. "Ya mean to tell me, ya killed my wife and sold my baby for a piddling two hundred dollars?"

Judas uncrossed his legs, slamming his foot down hard on the rickety floor. The remaining windowpane rattled. "Two hundred dollars was a lot of money back then. Two hundred dollars made it possible fer me to get by while I waited for my own son to be born." He pointed to Pete who was now standing just inside the bedroom door.

"He's my pride and joy. Knowing I had a son waiting fer me when I got out of prison was what kept me goin'. Course, it wasn't in my plans to get caught and sent to prison. I would'a rather raised my son myself. We could'a made a lot of money together."

Without warning, Dawson lashed out with a burst of vented-up anger, slamming his fist down hard on the table. A cloud of dust particles flew into the air, mingling with the rays of sunlight, which had made their way through the dead and dying limbs of a massive oak tree, directly across the yard from the missing back door.

"I would'a liked to have raised my son too!" Dawson shouted. "I would'a liked to have spent the last forty years with my wife. I would'a liked teachin' my son to play ball, took him fishin' and huntin', seen that he got a good education. But no! Ya stole all that from me. You're nothing but a low-down dirty piece of dog crap, not worth scraping off my shoe."

As soon as Dawson hit the table with his fist, Pete pointed the gun directly at him. Judas held up his hand to Pete, letting him know there was no real problem. "It's okay, son. He has ever' right to be mad with me. Not that I care, but he does have the right."

Pete lowered his gun. "Paw, I'm getting hungry. What we gonna eat fer breakfast?"

Judas slid his chair back from the table and looked angrily at his son. "Is that all ya ever think 'bout is food?" He pointed around the room. "Do ya see any food, son? I don't. How should I know what we gonna eat?"

"I could go down to Patsy's Kitchen there in Marbury," Pete suggested. "She's a good cook. Me and my old paw used to eat there sometimes."

Judas jumped to his feet, knocking the chair he was sitting in over backward. "Son, ya ain't got the sense God gave a flea-bit dog. The law is lookin' fer us. The last place ya want to be is in an eatin' place. I swear, if I didn't know better, I'd think your mama done got with another man and ya ain't my boy a'tall."

For the first time, Dawson suddenly saw a change come over Pete.

"My mama was a good woman. She was good to me. She used to make me fried baloney and egg sandwiches fer breakfast. They was good too. I could eat a whole pile of 'em 'bout now."

Judas started laughing. "Boy, your real mama never made ya no fried nothin'. I killed your real mama. The woman ya think was your mama is a cousin of mine."

Pete looked confused. "Ya killed my real mama?"

Dawson saw a slim chance to turn the tables on Judas. "That's right, Pete. Judas raped your real mama. Then nine months later, he killed her and took ya from her womb just like he killed my wife and took my son. Now he's turnin' you into a killer and a baby kidnapper. Thanks to him, you'll be spending the rest of your life either runnin' from the law or sittin' in prison."

Without warning, Judas drew back his fist and struck Dawson a hard blow alongside his head, knocking over his chair and landing him on the floor.

"Shut your sorry mouth!" Judas screamed as he kicked Dawson squarely in the ribs. "Ain't none of this your business. Pete is my boy, and he'll do as I say, or I'll put a whoopin' on him like he ain't never had before."

Dawson looked up. Judas was standing over him. "You're a sorry excuse for a father, Judas Solomon. A sorry excuse for a father."

Angered by his remarks, Judas kicked him again. Dawson tried to catch his leg to trip him, but the blow to his side was so hard it took his breath away. The last thing Dawson remembered was being struck in the head with the butt of Judas's gun. When he awoke sometime later, his hands were bound behind him, his feet held together with rope, his mouth covered with duct tape, and his head hurt badly. Dried blood covered the front of his shirt. His ribs and stomach felt like he'd been kicked by an irate mule. It was dark, except for the few rays of light piercing through the cracks between the boards of the building where he had been imprisoned. It was obvious he was no longer inside the house. He could feel and smell the cold damp ground beneath him. He looked at his surroundings. Rotted wood was stacked waist high in one corner. A rusty axe was leaned against the wall next to the wood. *Could that be the same axe that had killed my wife*, he thought. The smell of lighter wood filled his nostrils. He was obviously in the woodshed. His mouth was so dry his tongue stuck to the roof of his mouth. He tried to pull it open, but the duct tape wouldn't budge. He tried to move, but the rope, which held him to the chair, was so tight it dug into the flesh on his arms. A sharp pain passed through him and everything went blank once again.

After securing Dawson and placing him in the woodshed, Pete started in on Judas about the hunger pains gnawing at his stomach. "Paw, I need somethin' to eat. My stomach is growlin' like an old grizzly bear."

Judas slammed his fist down hard on the table. "What am I supposed to do 'bout it?" he yelled. "Do I look like a grocery store?"

"But, Paw."

"Don't but paw me, boy! I ain't got no food. If ya want somethin' to eat, go kill ya a squirrel. Just don't make no noise doin' it. The law might still be 'round here."

Pete looked puzzled. "How can I kill a squirrel without shootin' it, Paw?"

"I don't care how ya do it. Just don't make no racket doin' it."

Pete looked at Judas one last time before heading out the back door. "All right, Paw, if'n ya say so."

After Pete was gone, Judas leaned back in his chair, closed his eyes, and soon drifted off to sleep. When he awoke, it was dark inside the house. *Did I sleep all day?* he wondered. He looked around the room, but Pete was nowhere to be seen. "Confound it!" he yelled. "Where the heck is that boy?"

Somewhat confused and angry, Judas got up and looked out the window. All he could see were the thick woods that surrounded the house. As he was peering into the darkness, a queer feeling came over him, making the hair on the back of his neck stand on end. Judas was not one to scare easily. However, whatever was making him shake in his boots was also making him want to run like an old black cat with his tail on fire. Turning around slowly, he caught a glimpse of something moving across the room.

"Is 'at you, Pete?" he called out. "Answer me, boy. Is 'at you?"

There was no answer.

Judas reached for his shotgun, but it was gone. His mind began racing. *Who did I see? Where is my gun? Did the law get Pete?*

Cautiously, he began moving toward the backdoor when a vaguely familiar sounding voice called out to him. "Hello, Silas." Judas stopped dead in his tracks. No one had called him Silas for nearly forty years.

"Who's thar'?"

Suddenly, total darkness fell across the room as a dense gray blanket of clouds crept across the sky, making it impossible to see even his hand in front of his face. The room turned cold, a chill ran up his spine.

Again, the came eerie voice called out to him.

"What's the matter, Silas? Don't ya remember me?"

Judas wanted to run, but he was frozen with fear. "What ya want with me?"

"I just want to share my food with ya. Like I did forty years ago."

"No! Go away!" he pleaded.

A ghostly figure passed across the doorway leading into the front room where the bloody body of Sudie Huett had been discovered forty years earlier. Her once sweet, innocent voice whirled in and around the three-room house, leaving her words to echo in his mind.

"Go away? Why, Silas? Ain't ya hungry? Don't ya want some biscuits and a hot cup of coffee?"

Suddenly, the smell of hot biscuits and fresh made coffee filled his nostrils. His eyes searched the dark room looking for any sign of life. There was none. Judas could feel the hair on his arms rising as cold chills ran down his back. Sweat beads appeared on his forehead and then ran down the deep crease along the edge of his weathered leathery face. His deep-set eyes widened as he searched the blackness for the terror lurking in the shadows of his mind. Minutes crept by like a slow moving cloud on a windless day. Judas wanted to call out, but his voice stuck in his throat like a bloodthirsty tick on a sleeping dog. He tried to run, but his legs were too weak to carry the weight of his wiry body.

All at once, out of the darkest realm of existence, a looming, highlighted silhouette appeared. It was the figure of a woman with piercing blue eyes. Her hair pulled back from her face with wispy pieces of dainty curls framing her small delicate face. She was dressed in a blue print dress with a lace collar around the neck. Judas could feel his heart pounding in his chest. His knees began to tremble. A knot formed in the pit of his stomach.

"It can't be!" he exclaimed.

"Oh…but it is, Silas. It's me, Sudie Hubert."

Judas suddenly felt lightheaded. He dropped to his knees. "Where did ya come from?"

"I came from the ashes in the fireplace. Remember, Silas. That's where ya threw me after ya shot me, cut me open, and stole my baby."

"It can't be, you're dead!"

"That's right, Silas. I'm dead. Forced to remain here in this forgotten place until my death has been avenged"

Judas rubbed his rough calloused hands across his unbelieving eyes.

"So am I," a feeble voice called out from the room where Stella and John once lived.

Judas looked into the adjoining room. Just inside the door, he saw the figure of another woman. Her hair was long, dark, and stringy. In her eyes was a blank stare like that of a deadly shark. She was pacing back and forth across the room mumbling to herself.

"Now ya can hear the voices too. Don't ya, Silas?" she teased hauntingly.

Judas dropped his head, covering his eyes with his hands. "Stop! This is not happening. It's a dream. Leave me alone!" he yelled.

"Leave ya alone?" This time it was yet a different voice altogether calling out to him. "Ya didn't leave me alone, did ya, Silas? It wasn't enough that ya raped me. Ya had to come back and take the baby ya planted inside me."

Judas reluctantly opened his eyes. Before him stood the ghostly figure of Ginny Macon, the mother of his son.

"How can this be?" he cried. "You're dead too! You're all dead. Go away! Leave me alone! Please…Go away…all of ya. Just go away."

Within minutes the darkened room was filled with the ectoplasm of the women whose lives Judas Silas Solomon had so freely taken from them. Closer and closer they came, hovering over him, choking off the oxygen from the air around him. He could feel their cold clammy fingers touching him and clawing at his body. The room became cold like the middle of winter. His body shivered violently. His breath became labored. His heart raced, pounding in his chest like a jackhammer against unrelenting concrete. Moments later, he collapsed onto the floor, his knees drawn up tightly to his chest. He could feel the apparitions tearing at his soul, sucking the life force from him. As the last ounce of breath seeped from his body, he let out a bloodcurdling scream. Judas Silas Solomon was no more.

Sunlight returned to the room. The beautiful redbirds in the tree at the edge of the porch busied themselves building their nests. Squirrels scampered around the yard in search of food. A patch of yellow daffodils growing at the front of the house opened their blooms, welcoming the warmth of the sun.

Jake reached the intersection to the Marbury turnoff just before seven. The roadblock was still in place. A line of cars and logging trucks were stopped on both the north and southbound lanes. Ahead, the two deputies were busy checking people's credentials. It was obvious they had not found the men they were looking for. After several minutes,

Jake pulled up alongside Deputy Carson and handed him his license.

"Good morning," he said to the deputy. "Say, you didn't happen to see my dad come through here last night? His name is Dawson Hubert. Big fellow. Middle aged, dark hair."

Deputy Carson leaned his elbow on the edge of Jake's window. "As a matter of fact, we did. It was along about one, maybe two this morning. We talked a little about his wife's murder. He was telling us the suspect who killed her was known only by the name of Silas. Turns out the man we're looking for is Judas Silas Solomon."

Jake felt a knot form in the pit of his stomach. He'd seen the name Judas S. Solomon on his reports a hundred times, yet he had never connected it as being the same person who had possibly killed his mother. *How could I have missed that?* he thought.

"Did my father say which way he was going?"

"No, sir, but I do remember he turned right on twenty headed toward the school."

"Thanks."

"You have a good day, Mr. Tillery," said the deputy as he waved him on his way.

Joe Durden, the owner of the D&D Gas Station on the corner of Highway 31 and County Road 20, was out front turning on the gas pumps for the day. Jake looked at his fuel gauge and realized he should get the car filled with gasoline before venturing onward. Once through the intersection, he turned left into the parking lot and parked in front of the pumps.

"Good morning," Joe called to him. "Quite a mess they've got there, ain't it? I hear they're looking for the two men who killed that old man from Verbena. It's a shame. Folks these days ain't got no respect for life anymore."

Jake turned the ignition key to the off position, got out of his car, removed his gas cap, inserted the nozzle, and started the pump. "I'm looking for my dad, Dawson Hubert. You wouldn't happen to know him, would you?"

"Dawson Hubert, ya say. Yeah, I know a Dawson Hubert. Ain't seen him in years. He moved away from here after his wife was killed. Tragic. She was pregnant. Cut the baby right out'a her. They never did find it. The whole community was in an uproar." He paused as though he was collecting his thoughts. "Did you say Dawson is yo'r daddy?"

"Yes, I did." Jake extended his hand. "I'm Jake Tillery."

Joe shook his hand and introduced himself, "Joe Durden."

"Glad to meet you, Mr. Durden."

"Call me Joe. Ever'body else does."

"My dad didn't happen to come by here last night, did he?"

"No, I can't say he did." He paused. "Didn't ya say your name is Jake Tillery?"

"That's right."

"Well, if Dawson is your daddy, how come your last name ain't Hubert?"

"I'm that baby they never found."

For a few moments, Joe stood motionless as though he was in shock. "H-h-how? Wh-wh-when?" he stuttered.

Jake felt he needed to explain. "I believe the man they're looking for, Judas Solomon, is the same person who killed my mother. He took me from her womb and sold me on the black market to the people who became my adoptive parents. Only by chance was I able to find out what really happened. Do you remember the murder of Ginny Macon? It was around the same time as my mother's murder."

Joe thought for a moment. "Wasn't she that young woman who was raped and then murdered nine months later?"

"That's the one. Judas was the one who raped her. Then he waited for nine months to murder and steal her baby. Fortunately, he was captured shortly thereafter and convicted of her murder."

"What happened to the baby?"

"He was raised by some of Judas's kinfolks. When Judas was released from prison a few months back, he came back here, got up with his boy, Pete, and started his crime spree all over again."

"That's quite a story. Sounds like something from a dime store murder mystery."

He paused. "Say. Pete wouldn't be that boy whose folks owned a pig farm over 'round Verbena, would he?"

The pump clicked off. Jake removed the nozzle from the tank and replaced the gas cap. He took out his wallet and handed Joe two twenty-dollar bills. "Yes. He's the one all right."

Jake thought about telling Joe the whole story about Vicky's rescue and their new babies, but he also knew he needed to find his father as soon as possible.

"By the way, you wouldn't happen to know how to get to the house where my mother and daddy lived, would you?"

Joe folded the money and tucked it in his shirt pocket. "Sure I do. It's just off County Road 337. Go north about three miles. Take a right. Go about three or four miles east till ya come to 337 and take another right. It's somewhere there on that dirt road. I 'pect the house is gone by now. Ain't nobody lived in it since the murder. Folks claimed it was haunted." He paused. "Course I don't much believe in ghosts."

Jake got back into his car. "Neither do I," he agreed. However, something inside him told Jake he should try and find the old house. He was sure it would be one of the places his father would look. "Thanks for the info, Joe."

Joe placed a stack of blue paper towels in the windshield washer box. "You bet. Good luck finding your mother's killer. She was a sweet lady. Such a shame, her murder and all."

As Jake drove back onto Highway 31, he was much more interested in finding his father than he was his mother's killer. He was worried about Dawson and what he might do if he did find Judas, or worse, what Judas might do to him.

Beth, Mama Cora, and Kayleen arrived back at the hospital around two that afternoon. The window to the nursery was open, so the three women peered through the glass at the beautiful twin babies.

"Aren't they the prettiest little babies you've ever seen?" said Kayleen.

Mama Cora grinned proudly. "They surely are, Kayleen. The boy looks just like Dawson when he was a baby."

"I think the little girl looks like Vicky," said Beth.

Kayleen looked down the hallway. "I can't believe Papa and Jake aren't here to look at them. I wonder why. Surely, Jake's found Papa by now. They should be here."

Beth was worried too. She knew her daddy had a bad temper, especially when it came to protecting his family.

"Look," said Mama Cora, "there's Tina's baby over there. He's a handsome little fellow too."

"Where's Lyndsay's baby?" asked Kayleen.

"She's over there in the corner under that light. It looks like she might be a little jaundiced."

"Is she going to be all right?"

Mama Cora patted Kayleen on the back. "She'll be fine."

"I'm worried," said Beth.

"Me too, Mama?" added Kayleen.

Mama Cora interjected, "Not to worry, jaundice is a common condition for some newborns. Nothing to be worried about."

"No, Mama. I'm worried about Jake and Daddy. I thought for sure they'd be here when we got back."

"Maybe they're in the ward with the girls," answered Mama Cora.

A pediatric nurse came over to the window and began closing the curtain. Beth, Mama Cora, and Kayleen waved good-bye to the babies and then walked down the hall to the room where the mothers had been assigned. When they went inside, they were expecting to see Dawson and Jake. Instead, they saw Tom, Terry, and Detective Crawford. Detective Crawford was the first to speak.

"Good morning, ladies."

"Hello, Detective," replied Beth.

"You ladies wouldn't happen to know where Dawson and Jake are, would you?"

"I was hoping you'd know," answered Beth. "Dad left last night. He said he was going to help find Judas and Pete. Jake left before sunup to look for Dad. We haven't seen nor heard from them since."

Detective Crawford laid out a map of the area on one of the food tables. "We've combed every inch of northern Autauga and southern Chilton counties looking for Judas and Pete. It's as though the two of them just dropped off the face of the earth."

"And ya ain't seen my boys neither?" asked a now worried Mama Cora.

"No, I'm sorry to say I haven't."

Beth began pacing back and forth in front of the big picture window with a panoramic view of the parking lot. "Where on earth could they be?"

Detective Crawford pointed to the Verbena area. "This is the pig farm where Solomon and Pete were known to be last. However, I'm thinking they're probably in Georgia by now. We've alerted every law enforcement agency between here and Atlanta. Someone is bound to see them sooner or later."

"What about Papa and Uncle Jake?" asked Kayleen. "Where are they?"

"I'm sure we'll find them too," assured the detective as he turned to Mama Cora. "Mrs. Hubert, can you show me on this map the location of the house where your daughter-in-law was murdered?"

Mama Cora looked at the map. "It's just off this road here," she answered, pointing to County Road 337.

"I believe we went down that road yesterday, but I don't remember seeing any houses. It was mostly just woods."

"After Sudie was killed, the folks that lived along that road moved away. The land there wasn't much good for farming. I used to tell my husband all it was good for was to hold the earth together. I don't 'pect the house is even there anymore. I even heard tell folks claimed to have seen a ghost what looked like Sudie roaming around in thar'."

"Mama!" exclaimed Beth. "That's ridiculous. There's no such things as ghosts."

Mama Cora put her hands on her hips and cocked her body to one side. "Tell that to folks that seen 'em."

Beth looked at Kayleen and just shook her head.

Detective Crawford folded the map and placed it back inside his coat pocket. "I'm going back to Mountain Creek to see if I can find Dawson and Jake. You folks stay close to a phone. I'll call as soon as I hear anything."

As Detective Crawford was about to exit the room, Vicky called out to him, "Please, Jim, find my husband and father-in-law. I can't raise two little babies by myself. They need a daddy."

"Try not to worry, Vicky," replied the detective. "I'm sure they're fine. When I find them, I'll tell them you said to get their butts back here where they belong."

Vicky smiled. "Thanks, Jim. You do that."

12

Déjà Vu

Jake found County Road 23 and turned right. Three miles down the road, he saw a rusty sign dangling from a metal post. The words CR 337 were barely legible. He turned right onto the narrow, red-clay dirt road. It was as if time had forgotten the road was ever there. Huge trees hung over the road forming a tunnel, their branches intermingling like lovers, their bodies embracing. There were wide ruts in the road where rain had washed away all signs of life. He had to drive slowly in order to maneuver around them. As he drove, he looked for any sign of a house. Halfway down the road, Jake looked to his left. There among the trees and overgrown bushes stood the skeletal remains of an old house. He would have missed seeing it if not for the crumbling chimney that towered above the undergrowth. He stopped the car, got out, and began making his way through the dense growth of scrubs and plants.

When he reached the edge of the porch, he stopped dead in his tracks. Something inside him left him feeling like he'd been here before. He knew instinctively he was at the right house. Carefully, he made his way up the half-rotted steps and across the dilapidated porch. He pushed aside the front door that hung loosely on a single hinge and stepped inside. The room was exactly like Stella had described it to him. Here was the place where his mother and father had once lived, loved, and shared their lives. An eerie feeling crept up his spine like a spider creeping across its web. Slowly, he crossed the room. When he reached the door leading into the kitchen, he was shocked by what he saw. There on the floor lay the man he knew to be Judas Solomon. He was lying in a fetal position. The look on his face was that of pure terror.

Jake immediately knelt down and checked for a pulse. There was none. It was obvious he'd been dead for several hours. His body was cold and stiff. What Jake found to be strange was the dead man's hair. It was totally white. *What could have happened to him?* he wondered. There was no blood. No signs of being beaten or stabbed. He decided he needed to alert the sheriff right away. However, something inside him told him he should look further into the situation. When he stood up, he could see out the back door and into the yard. When he spotted the woodshed, he decided to check it out.

Jake stepped over the body and carefully made his way out the back door. Near the door was an old well. Jake walked over to it. A dark stain on the curbing told him this was his mother's blood. He touched it. A cold chill ran through his body. *This is where Judas stood when he washed the blood from the axe*, he thought. *How would my life have been different had my mother not been murdered? Where would I be now? Life after any murder is never the same, not just for the family involved, but also for those who simply knew of the victim or their family members.*

As he pondered these thoughts, a noise from the woodshed drew his attention. Cautiously, he walked toward the small, rundown, wood plank building. As he got closer, he could hear a moaning sound coming from inside it. *It could be Pete*, he thought, *or it could be Dawson.* Either way, he had to find out. Since he had no weapon, he picked up a rusty old shovel that was leaned against the side of the shed. Heedful of the possible danger he might encounter, he slowly and carefully pushed open the door to the shed. It was dark inside. The only light was from the rays of sunlight peeking through the cracks between the boards. He stepped inside. As his eyes adjusted to the light, he could tell there was someone lying on the dirt floor. He soon realized it was his father. He dropped the shovel and quickly went to his side. He began by removing the duct tape from Dawson's mouth.

"Dad!" Are you all right?"

Dawson had never been more glad to see his son than he was at that moment. "I'm fine, but I think I might have a couple of cracked ribs."

Jake loosened the ropes from Dawson's hands and feet. "What in the world happened?"

"I let my guard down and got nabbed by Solomon and his boy. Where are they now? Are they gone?"

Jake helped Dawson to his feet. "Well, Dad, I don't know about Pete, but Solomon is dead."

Dawson was astonished. "What? Did ya kill 'em?"

"No. I found him on the kitchen floor. He's been dead for some time."

With help from Jake, Dawson slowly got to his feet. "Unbelievable. I have to see for myself."

Jake helped his father get back to the house. When they entered the kitchen, Dawson could hardly believe his eyes.

"By the look on his face, I'd say something or someone scared the living daylights out'a him," Dawson remarked.

"That's what I thought too. Look at his hair. It's completely white. You don't reckon Pete killed him, do you?"

Dawson thought back to last night's goings-on. "Well, last night I told Pete about how his real mother died. He looked upset but not so much that he would kill his paw. As much as anything, I think he was afraid of him."

"Well, somebody did the world a favor."

"Ya got that right."

For the first time, Jake noticed the swelling over Dawson's right eye. "Dad, we need to get you to the hospital to get checked out. We also need to get to a phone so we can let Detective Crawford know about Judas."

Dawson smiled. "You're right, Jake. Let's go see our babies too."

At the same time Dawson and Jake got to Jake's car, Detective Crawford pulled up alongside them.

"Looks like you've been hit by a Mack Truck," he called out the window to Dawson.

Dawson touched his forehead and shook his head in agreement.

Jake pointed toward the house. "You'll find Judas in the kitchen. He's dead."

"Who killed him?"

"I have no idea," answered Dawson.

Jake intervened, "I found him lying on the floor dead as a doorknob. He looks like he'd seen a ghost. Dad was tied up in the woodshed. We thought it might have been Pete that killed him since he's nowhere to be found."

"Oh, we found him all right," said Detective Crawford jokingly. "He was at Patsy's Kitchen. He'd done ordered him a big breakfast and was about to eat it when one of the deputies walked in. He arrested him on the spot. All he could say was, he was hungry and couldn't he eat his breakfast before they hauled him off to jail."

"Well, sir, ain't that somethin'?" said Dawson. "I guess it's over and done with now. Judas is dead and Pete's behind bars. I just wish we knew who killed Judas. I'd shore like to shake his hand."

Detective Crawford had a slightly crooked smirk on his face. "Well, Dawson, to coin a phrase from the movie *Gone with the Wind* and my favorite character in the movie, Rhett Butler, 'Frankly, Scarlet, I don't give a damn.' I'm just glad he won't be around to kill anyone else. He caused a lot of grief to a lot of people during his lifetime."

"He ain't worth frettin' over, that's for sure," added Dawson.

Jake placed his hand on his father's shoulder. "I agree, Dad. A man's life after he commits murder ain't worth crying over. So let's go see those pretty babies now."

Author's Note

Writers often use a real-life subject as a basis for the books they write, and so it was with my first murder mystery, Murder at Mountain Creek. The victim was my cousin. Her real name was Scunnie Newman Huett. She was married to my blood cousin, Dempsey Huett. Her murder took place shortly after I was born, in 1951. Through the years, the story of her death was told and retold among the members of my family.

The events surrounding the morning of her death were written as close to the actual murder as I could possibly write. However, one must understand, I was only a baby myself when the murder took place, therefore, the only people who could possibly know what actually took place were Scunnie, her eighteen-month old baby, Linda, and of course, the killer.

The thing that bothered me most about the murder was the disappearance of the baby Scunnie carried. As a writer and a soft-hearted human being, I wanted the story to have a happy ending; an ending that rarely exists in murder mysteries. The only way to give the story a somewhat happy ending was to have the baby live and later found alive and well. As I have said many times, when doing personal appearances, Murder at Mountain Creek was my book, its content from Scunnie's death forward was honed from my imagination, therefore, I could make it end as I saw fit.

Those of you who have read Murder at Mountain Creek knows how it ends. Those of you who have not read it, I recommend you do so before you read Life After Murder. When doing so, remember, the tragic murder of the beloved, Scunnie Huett was real, the circumstances following her death were strictly my imagination.

In my story, Jake was the baby no one knew existed and I suppose there could very well be someone out there who is real, who does exist. Chances are no one will ever know. However, if he or she does exist, I hope he or she has had a good life and is working on a happy ending.